ERETH'S BIRTHDAY

Avi

SIMON AND SCHUSTER

SIMON AND SCHUSTER

This edition published in Great Britain by Simon & Schuster UK Ltd, 2006
First published in Great Britain in hardback, 2003, by Simon & Schuster UK Ltd
A Viacom company

1 3 5 7 9 10 8 6 4 2

Simon & Schuster UK Ltd
Africa House
64-78 Kingsway
London WC2B 6AH

A CIP catalogue record for this book is available from the British Library

ISBN 0-689-83720-8

Printed and bound in Great Britain by Cox & Wyman Ltd, Reading, Berkshire

For Elise, Beth and Ruth

CONTENTS

I

A Special Day

In Dimwood Forest, in the dark, smelly log where the old porcupine Erethizon Dorsatum lived, Ereth — as he preferred to call himself — woke slowly.

Not the sweetest smelling of creatures, Ereth had a flat face with a blunt, black nose and fierce, grizzled whiskers. As he stirred, he rattled his sharp — if untidy — quills, flexed his claws, yawned, frowned, and grumbled, "Musty moose marmalade," only to suddenly remember what day it was and smile. Today was his birthday.

Ereth had given very little thought to what *he* would do about the day. As far as he was concerned, his birthday meant others would be doing something for *him*. And the one he was quite certain would be doing all the providing was his best friend, Poppy.

Poppy, a deer mouse, lived barely an acorn toss from Ereth's log in a grey, lifeless tree — a snag with a hole on one side. She resided there with her husband, Rye, and their eleven children.

Ereth, in a *very* private sort of way, loved Poppy.

He had never told anyone about this love, not even her. Enough for him to live near her. But since the porcupine was certain that Poppy thought of him as her best friend, he assumed she would be making a great fuss over his birthday. A party, certainly. Lavish gifts, of course. Best of all, he would be the centre of attention.

So it was that when Ereth waddled out of his log that morning he was surprised not to find Poppy waiting for him. All he saw were her eleven children playing about the base of the snag, squeaking and squealing uproariously.

"Why can't young folks ever be still?" A deeply disappointed Ereth complained to himself. "Potted pockets of grizzly grunions, it would save so much trouble if children were born . . . old."

Agitated, he approached the young mice. "Where's your mother?" he barked. "Where's your wilted wet flower of a father?"

"They . . . went . . . looking for . . . something," one of them said.

Though Ereth's heart sank, he made a show of indifference by lifting his nose scornfully and moving away from the young mice.

Snowberry, one of the youngsters, glanced anxiously around at the others, then cried out, "Good morning, Uncle Ereth!"

This greeting was followed by the ten other young mice singing out in a ragged, squeaky chorus, "Good morning, Uncle Ereth!"

Ereth turned and glowered at the youngsters. "What the tiddlywink toes do you want?" he snapped.

"Aren't you going to stay and play with us, Uncle Ereth?" Snowberry called.

"No!"

"Why?"

"I'm . . . busy."

"You don't look busy."

"I'm trying to find some peace and quiet," Ereth snapped. "With all the noise you make, buzzard breath, what else do you think I'd be doing?"

One of the mice — her name was Columbine — slapped a paw over her mouth in order to keep from laughing out loud.

Ereth glared at her. "What are you laughing at?"

"You," Columbine sputtered. "You always say such funny things!"

"Listen here, you smidgen of slipper slobber,"

Ereth fumed. "Don't tell *me* I talk funny. Why don't you stuff your tiny tail into your puny gullet and gag yourself before I flip you into some skunk-cabbage sauce and turn you into a pother of butterfly plunk?"

Instead of frightening the young mice, Ereth's outburst caused them to howl with glee. Sassafras laughed so hard he fell down and had to hold his stomach. "Uncle Ereth," he cried, "you are so hilarious! Please say something else!"

"Belching beavers!" Ereth screamed. "I am not hilarious! You're just a snarl of runty seed suckers with no respect for anyone older than you. How about a little consideration? As far as I'm concerned you mice have as much brains as you could find in a baby bee's belly button."

"But you *are* funny, Uncle Ereth," cried another of the young mice, whose name was Walnut. "Nobody else talks like you do. We love it when you swear and get angry at us."

"I am not angry!" Ereth raged. "If I were angry, I'd turn you all into pink pickled pasta so fast it would make lightning look like a slow slug crawling up a slick hill. So listen up, you tub of tinsel twist."

This was too much for the young mice. They

laughed and squeaked till their sides ached.

"Uncle Ereth," said Sassafras between giggles, "please — *please* — say something funny again. You are the funniest animal in the whole forest!"

Staring wrathfully at the young mice, Ereth considered uttering something unbelievably disgusting — dangling doggerels — thought better of it, and wheeled about, heading north as fast as he could.

"Uncle Ereth!" the mice shouted after him. "Please stay and say something else funny. *Please* don't go!"

But Ereth refused to stop.

Sassafras watched the porcupine plunge into the forest, then turned to the others. "But what are we going to tell Mum and Dad?" he cried. "They told us to make sure he didn't go anywhere."

"Oh, don't worry," Columbine assured her brother. "Uncle Ereth always comes back."

2
Ereth Makes a Decision

"Kids," Ereth muttered as he hurried away. "They think they're so wonderful. Truth is, they do nothing but make their elders work hard, eat their food, ask for things, break them, then proclaim all adults stupid! And what do kids give in return? Nothing!

"All that baby-sitting I do . . . all that listening to their endlessly boring stories, dumb jokes, what they learned today . . . hearing Poppy and Rye talk about this one's problems, that one's doings . . . attending their parties . . . finding presents for them . . .

"Well, here it is, *my* birthday. At least I only have one a year. But do those kids notice? No! Not so much as a gill of grasshopper gas. Do they care what I feel, think, am? Not one pinch of pith pills! Right! The whole world would be better off without kids. So all I say is, keep kids to the rear, blow wind, and turn on the fan!"

With such thoughts and words churning in his mind, Ereth rushed on. Once, twice, he passed a rabbit, a squirrel, a vole, but when they saw the mood the porcupine was in they retreated quickly, not willing even to call a greeting. After all, the creatures of Dimwood Forest knew Erethizon Dorsatum quite well. Very few had any desire to interfere with him when he was in one of his bad moods — which was clearly the case that morning.

The old porcupine pressed on, his mind taken up by a careful composition of the things he hated, the insults he had endured, the slights he had suffered. The list was very long. The more he recalled, the grumpier he became, and the faster he hurried on.

It was an hour before Ereth allowed himself to pause. All his emotion and running had quite worn him out and made him ravenous. Spying a young pine tree, he scrambled over to it and began to peel away the outer bark, then chew on the green layer under-neath.

"Good, good," he babbled as he gobbled. "This is more like it."

Suddenly he lifted his nose, sniffed, and frowned. "Squirrel-splat soup! The air has changed."

It was true — the air *was* different. It had become crisp and had a deep, tangy smell. And now that Ereth thought about it, the days had been growing shorter, the nights longer. It was only a question of when the first snow would arrive.

"Seasons," Ereth thought to himself. "Boiled bat butter! Just when you get used to one way, everything changes. Why can't things ever stay the way they are? Phooey and fried salamander spit with a side order of rat ribbon. I hate change!"

More than ever, Ereth was convinced that he needed *something* to mark the day. But what? It had to be something special. Something just for him. Then, in a flash, he knew exactly what would please him most. *Salt.*

Just to think about salt turned Ereth's longing into deep desire and dreamy drools. For Ereth, salt was the most delicious food in the whole world. He could shut his eyes and almost taste it. Oh, if only he had a chunk! A piece! Even a *lick* of salt would salvage the day. No, there was nothing he would not do for the smallest bit of it.

The old porcupine sighed. Since no one else was going to pay attention to him, he owed it to himself to find *some* birthday treat, and salt was the perfect thing. But where was he going to find any?

Though Ereth, with his great knowledge of Dimwood Forest, knew exactly where *he* was, finding salt was quite another matter. He considered New Farm, a place where some humans kept a whole block of salt in the middle of a lawn. Once, when the block had shattered and fallen to the ground, Ereth had gorged himself for days. Though truly fabulous, that salt was long gone. Moreover, when the humans replaced the block they put it at a height convenient for deer — not porcupines.

"Deer dainties!" Ereth snarled with contempt. "Why couldn't they have put the salt out for *me*?"

So the question remained, Where could Ereth find salt?

Then Ereth remembered: on the far northern side of Dimwood Forest was a lake. Long Lake, the animals called it. On its shore humans had built a log cabin. Rather crudely constructed, it did not even sit on the earth, but on a platform a few feet off the ground. The cabin was used rarely, only when humans wanted to hunt or trap animals. Every year brought frightening stories of deer, fox, and rabbits, among others, being killed, hurt, or maimed by these humans. Hardly a wonder that the cabin — though more often than not deserted — was a place the animals of Dimwood Forest avoided. Just thinking about it made Ereth shudder. And yet . . .

As Ereth also knew, these humans often left traces of salt on the things they used. Sometimes it was nothing more than a smear of sweat on the handle of a tool, a canoe paddle, or an odd bit of clothing like a hatband. These objects were often stored in that space beneath the cabin.

Scanty though these tastings were, they were tempting enough for Ereth to venture to the log cabin now and again to satisfy his salt cravings. Once he had been rewarded by finding an almost full bag of salty crisps. That was a day to remember.

Hardly a wonder then, that just the possibility of finding even a lick of salt stirred Ereth.

He looked around. Overhead loomed the great trees that kept the ground dim and gave the forest its name. Such sky as he could see was grey, while the sun itself seemed to have turned dull. White mist curled up from the earth's murky nooks and crannies.

"It's almost winter," Ereth told himself. "This may be my last chance to get salt for a while. Besides," he reminded himself yet again, "it's my birthday. I deserve something special."

Even so, the porcupine hesitated, all too aware of the risks involved. Fooling around with humans, especially if they were hunters or trappers, was risky.

"Bug bubble gum," he swore. "What do I care if there are humans at the cabin? Nothing scares *me*."

With that thought Ereth continued making his way in a northerly direction towards Long Lake, the cabin, and the salt.

3

Marty the Pine Marten

As Ereth rushed on he passed beneath a particularly large oak tree. So quickly did he move by it, he had no notion that two dark eyes were looking down at him. The eyes belonged to Marty the pine marten.

About three feet in length, and more than a foot tall, Marty the pine marten had short, brown fur and small, round eyes almost blank of emotion. His legs were stubby but powerful. With his sharp claws he could climb trees and leap about branches as nimbly as a squirrel. On the ground he was just as agile.

The only thing Marty feared was humans. With reason. Human hunters, attracted by the pine marten's glossy brown fur, had all but exterminated his family. Marty was the only one left, a fact that filled him with enormous rage. Even so, he kept to a stern, self-imposed rule: never, ever tangle with humans. They were far too dangerous.

Though he killed birds — even ate their eggs — what Marty liked to hunt were other four-legged creatures, like mice, rats, rabbits, and squirrels.

Marty chose his victims with care, stalking them silently and patiently, wanting to be certain he could overwhelm them with the savagery of a single attack.

Once he chose his prey, Marty pursued it for however long it took to bring the creature down. It could be hours. It could be days. Or weeks. The most patient of hunters, Marty loved nothing more than to devise clever strategies to fool his victims, luring them into places where he could surprise them and they would be defenceless. Those whom he assaulted barely had time to know what hit them.

To further ensure his success Marty traveled alone, keeping to trees, rocks, and leaves, where his dark fur blended in. Such tactics made him almost invisible. Indeed, Marty was rarely seen — until it was too late.

Though he never bragged about it, never gloated, rarely even smiled — in fact, had almost nothing to do with any other creature — Marty's solitary tactics almost always worked.

Hardly a wonder that Marty gained the reputation for being the most patient hunter in all of

Dimwood Forest. Indeed, he rather liked to consider himself Death on four paws.

And of all the forest and woodland animals Marty hunted, it was porcupines he enjoyed hunting the most. It was not that porcupines had injured Marty in any way. They did not insult him. They did not compete for food or space. No, it was their vanity that infuriated Marty the pine marten. Porcupines believed that no one could interfere with their lives, that they could do whatever they wished. How dare any creature think itself immune from Marty's anger?

What's more, Marty had found a way to successfully attack porcupines. By careful observation, he had discovered that porcupines had no quills on their bellies. The belly was the porcupine's most vulnerable spot. If Marty picked his moment with care, moved with complete surprise, a porcupine could be successfully attacked from *below*.

Thus it was that whenever Marty came upon a porcupine, he liked nothing better than to hunt it down and kill it.

Hardly a wonder that when Marty the pine marten looked down from his perch in the old oak tree and saw old Ereth lumbering along beneath him, he became very excited.

"Ahhh," he whispered to himself. "It's Ereth! If ever there was a self-centred porcupine, he's the worst. Look at the way he's waddling along! Not a worry in the world. Acting as if he could live forever. Well, I'll teach him a thing or two!"

From that moment, Marty the pine marten began to stalk Ereth.

4
In Pursuit of Salt

The day grew colder. Not that Ereth cared. He rushed on, completely absorbed in the anticipated pleasures of salt. At times, his desire was so great he began to salivate, producing great drools of spit, which he sucked up noisily.

So focused were his thoughts on salt that he failed to notice when it began to snow. Coming with a breathless, hurried hush, the snow's silence was intense, swallowing every sound like a sponge absorbing water. Within moments, the entire forest became utterly still.

The snow was an inch deep before Ereth even realised it was there. Suddenly he could not see his own paws. Surprised, he gazed up. For just a moment Ereth imagined that it wasn't snow falling, but salt, and his heart leaped with joy. Then a particularly large flake of snow landed on his nose and made him sneeze. That brought him to his senses.

"Stupid snow," he complained. "You would think it would have the decency to wait until I got to where I was going before it started."

Though Ereth knew the snow would make travelling harder, not for a moment did he consider returning home. "What do I care?" he told himself. "It's my birthday. Who needs noisy mice? The salt will taste even better when I get there."

With an angry shake of his head — as if *that* could get rid of the snow — Ereth pushed on.

Leaping silently from tree branch to tree branch, Marty the pine marten followed.

The snow tumbled from the sky like confetti from a barrel. It sleeved tree branches in white. It hid rocks and stumps. It covered the land until its surface became round and soft, melding into one continuous undulating form. It was as if an enormous eraser were rubbing out the world, leaving nothing but one vast sheet of blank, white paper. Only Ereth, like a solitary, dark dot, moved across it.

Becoming weary, Ereth paused and looked back over his shoulder at the trail he was making. To his surprise it did not extend very far. Like a ghost, he left no tracks. The thought startled him. Then he realized it was only that the snow had covered his paw prints.

Shifting his gaze forwards, the porcupine tried to calculate how far he would have to go before he reached the cabin. A good way. Sighing with frustration, he told himself yet again that the salt would make his efforts worthwhile.

He went on.

The snow became so deep, it was increasingly difficult to keep his chin above the surface. "Elephant elbows," Ereth swore, beginning to falter for the first time. He glanced back. For just a second he thought something was following him. "Nonsense," he muttered. Reminding himself yet again of the tasty treat that lay ahead, he pushed on, one step at a time.

The sky grew darker, the air colder, the snow deeper. The trip was taking hours.

"Stop snowing!" Ereth shouted at the unrelenting sky. "Can't you see I'm trying to get some salt?"

There was no reply.

Pausing to catch his breath, Ereth began to

wonder if he would ever reach the cabin. As he recalled, the trail led over a small hill. Beyond that, right on the shores of Long Lake, was the cabin.

Perhaps he should go home. He turned to look back. Once again he had the brief sensation that something was stalking him. "You're acting like an old creature," Ereth chided himself. "Imagining things." And he moved on.

Marty the pine marten, high in a tree, seeing Ereth look back, ducked away in haste. He need not have bothered. Ereth merely glanced back before continuing on.

"Good," Marty muttered. "All I need to be is patient. *Very* patient."

"No," Ereth said under his breath as he trudged along. "I've come too far to go back." Besides, he reminded himself for the millionth time, it was his birthday. Back home there was nothing but raucous children. Better to be alone than in the midst of a crowd and ignored.

The porcupine did consider climbing a tree to wait out the storm. He shook his head. "I'm too close to salt."

On he went.

Ereth blinked open his eyes. Had he fallen asleep? Had he stopped? Had he walked in his sleep? If so, how far had he gone?

Ereth peered to the right and the left. The landscape revealed nothing. The forest was just as white as the last time he had looked. For all he knew he might have gone a mile. Or ten. Or perhaps he'd fallen asleep and hadn't moved at all. He looked back. Was something there? No. He was getting silly.

With a shake of his quills – sloughing off what felt like a ton of snow – Ereth forced himself forward again. But it had become very hard to walk. Perhaps, he told himself by way of encouragement, he was just climbing the hill, the last obstacle before reaching the cabin. He did know he was feeling light-headed. Hadn't he thought something was following him? Even so, he took one slow step after another slow step, like a wind-up toy running down.

Suddenly, his way seemed easier. Lifting his head Ereth looked forward. With the swirling snow in his eyes, it took a moment for him to realise he was looking down a hill, beyond which was an open space. At the bottom, Ereth saw a large mound of snow. In one or two places, light seemed to glow from within the mound. Sticking up from the top of the mound was a silver pipe, from which dark smoke drifted. The smoke carried the smell of roasting meat. Ereth, a vegetarian, curled his lips in disgust.

But the evidence was plain: the open space was Long Lake. Buried in the snow was the log cabin. The cabin would have salt. But inside the cabin were . . . *humans.*

5

The Cabin

There was almost no animal or bird in the world Ereth feared. Owls, foxes, beavers – they were all one to him. True, only rarely would any of them bother him. His sharp quills assured him of that. And if the need came, he was more than capable of defending himself.

Humans were quite another matter. Sometimes they merely watched the animals in the forest. Other moments they wanted to touch them. Or run away. On still other occasions, however, the humans stayed and killed. People were that unpredictable.

The last thing the tired Ereth wanted to do was confront one. Besides, if humans were in the cabin, most likely it was because they were hunting. No, it did not bode well at all. And yet, there was the salt . . .

Staring at the cabin, Ereth tried to make up his mind what to do.

❉

Marty the pine marten, perched high on a branch forty yards behind Ereth, looked on with troubled interest. He, too, realised that humans were in residence. As he had followed Ereth through the forest, Marty had wondered where the porcupine was so doggedly heading. Now that he saw the destination, he could guess what the porcupine was after. "Salt," Marty said to himself. "That stupid beast has come out in a storm in search of human salt."

Just to know he was close to humans made Marty anxious. He had little doubt these humans were hunters, the worst kind of humans from his point of view. For all he knew, they might even be looking for him, just as they had tracked down his whole family. It made him recall his ironclad rule: *keep far away from humans and all things human.*

"If Ereth has any brains," Marty thought, "he'll back off from that cabin and those people. I hope he does. He's acting tired. He's probably cold and hungry. Good! When he turns back from the cabin, he won't have the energy to resist when I strike.

"Of course, if he's idiot enough to go forward, I'll wait him out. There are always ways to lure someone like Ereth to where I'd like him to be."

Marty flexed his sharp claws, watched, and waited.

Ereth gave a shake of his head. There was, all in all, no choice to be made. He was cold, tired, and hungry. As far as he could determine, the best shelter would be directly under the cabin. Relatively speaking, it would be warm and dry there. It was probably the best place to find some food too. And of course, there was the whole purpose of the trip to consider: *salt*. How could he come so far without so much as a lick to show for it? Besides, though he did not like to mess with humans, he thought it most unlikely they would go under the house.

Moving downhill slowly, his breath a cloud of frosty vapour, Ereth watched and listened with every step he took. He was halfway there when, with a flash of golden light, the cabin door burst open. A man so bundled in furs he looked more bear than human stepped onto the porch, gathered up the last load of logs that lay by the door, then returned to the cabin. The door banged behind him, shutting in the light.

After a brief pause, Ereth continued downhill. Moving as fast as the deep snow and his short legs allowed, he waddled across the open space between hill and cabin. Heart racing, panting for breath, he ducked under the structure.

He was there. The heat radiating down from the house above was instantly soothing.

Ereth took a deep breath and looked around. Only a little snow had collected, and that on the northern side. He noticed a broken chair, a blue plastic tarpaulin bunched up in a corner, a canoe, a snowmobile, a pile of long logs, and, on the pile, an *axe*.

Unable to restrain himself, Ereth rushed forward, climbed the log pile, sniffed at the axe handle, and all but swooned. The axe handle bore the remains of human sweat: salt.

Heart aflutter, Ereth stuck out his tongue and began to lick the handle as a human would attack an ice cream cornet. Oh, rapture! Oh, bliss! Oh, *salt!* It was all he had imagined. The struggle through the snow had been worth it!

In a dreamy mood, he had just begun to chew on the axe handle when he was interrupted by the sound of a human voice from above.

"I'm telling you, Wayne," the voice said, "I'm so hungry I could eat a live porcupine!"

"Pulsating puppy pimples," Ereth snarled. "He can start by chewing my tail!"

Despite brave thoughts, Ereth, wondering if it might be better to bolt from the cabin while escape was still easy, looked around nervously. Though everything in him told him to run, the idea of doing *something* to teach that human a lesson was hard to resist.

Turning back to the axe handle, an angry Ereth gnawed furiously. As he chewed, he cast his eyes around in search of something else to mangle.

That's when he spied the snowmobile. Ereth was perfectly aware what it was. He had experienced just how much noise they made, the ghastly fumes they left in their wake, the way they chewed up the forest floor. Having seen them from a distance he also knew how humans used them: by sitting on the long black seat that ran down the middle, then twisting the handlebars, which caused the machine to shoot forward at enormously loud and smelly speeds.

Though Ereth did not like snowmobiles, humans, he knew, loved them. As far as he was concerned, that made the snowmobile the perfect target.

Having chewed the axe handle almost in two, the porcupine waddled over to the snowmobile. Using his front paws, he hoisted himself onto the black seat. It was soft and pliable. Twisting around, he lifted his tail and whacked it a few times. When he was done, a goodly number of quills remained sticking straight up from the seat. "Burping bird burgers," he muttered. "That'll fix them."

That accomplished, Ereth used his high perch to observe the rest of the area. In doing so he noticed a cardboard box and wondered if there was anything in it worth eating.

Climbing down from the snowmobile, he waddled over to the box and peered inside, only to recoil in fear. The box held four black, metal spring traps, the kind human trappers use to catch animals by their legs. There was also a box trap, designed to catch larger animals alive and transport them elsewhere.

"Killers," Ereth whispered in fury. "They're nothing but killers!"

"Hey, Parker," one of the human voices suddenly said from above. "We need to get some more firewood. Where'd you leave that axe?"

"Under the cabin. On the log pile."

"If we're going to keep from freezing tonight I'd better chop us some more wood. It's getting colder."

"Suits me."

"Fine," the voice said. "I'm going to get some wood from under the cabin. Be right back." The conversation was followed by the sound of one of the humans moving towards the cabin door.

Ereth, close to panic, looked for a place to conceal himself. He caught sight of the blue plastic tarpaulin off in a corner.

From above came more footsteps as well as the sound of a door opening and closing. Hurriedly Ereth clawed his way under the plastic.

6

Ereth's Revenge

From beneath the tarpaulin Ereth could see nothing. But he could hear someone stomp out onto the porch, then crunch through the snow around the cabin.

There were some grunts and groans, which Ereth presumed were the sounds of the human lifting one of the logs. For a moment all Ereth could hear was breathing. Then he heard a *snap,* followed by a cry: "Darn! Who did this?"

A smiling Ereth knew the man had tried to use the axe.

"Must have been a porcupine!" the man snarled.

Ereth grinned.

The human swearing was followed by the sound of steps that suggested the man was going back around the cabin to the porch.

Ereth poked his head out from under the plastic and listened intently. Within moments there came the sound of a human voice.

"Hey, Wayne! Some blazing idiot of a porcupine chewed through the axe handle. Broke on my first stroke. Can't use it."

"Oh, oh."

"And hey, man, with night coming on and the temperature dropping, we're going to run out of heat. Maybe we'd better head out while the going is good. Not much point in hanging around here anyway."

"What about the rest of the traps?"

"How many did we set? Sixteen out of twenty? Not bad, considering the weather. We can take care of the rest later."

"Just have to move quickly," the second man agreed. "Better not travel in the dark."

"Fine with me. We'll just leave everything and go."

Ereth, feeling quite satisfied with himself, retreated as far back under the tarpaulin as he could go.

For a while he heard footfalls crisscrossing directly overhead. These sounds were followed by movement on the porch and the sound of the humans crunching through the snow.

"Hey, Wayne," a voice called. "Give me a hand with the snowmobile."

Ereth heard sounds of pushing, and shoving and hauling.

"Come on, get on. We gotta move."

Ereth held his breath.

"Yooooooow!"

"What's the matter?"

"Holy . . . look at that! Porcupine quills! I sat on them! Ow!"

The other man laughed. "Hey, you said you could eat a porcupine alive, didn't you? Guess he heard what you said and got to you first."

"Yeah, right."

Ereth grinned and nodded.

There was a loud roar as the snowmobile's motor kicked in.

"You going to sit or stand?"

"Hurts too much to sit."

"Sure, but it'll hurt a lot more if you stand and fall off. I'll go as fast as I can."

The noise rose and fell as the snowmobile roared off. The stench of gas fumes made Ereth gag. Soon the machine — and the humans — were gone. The deep winter silence returned.

✳

From his place on the hill Marty the pine marten watched the snowmobile race away.

Though surprised, he was very pleased. "Good," he said to himself. "The humans are gone. Now if I can get Ereth away from the cabin, he'll be an easy target." He put his mind to finding a way to lure the porcupine back into the woods.

Beneath the cabin, Ereth waddled about sniffing, in hopes of finding something to eat. It was while lifting his nose up towards one corner of the cabin that he suddenly caught a powerful scent. *Salt.* Such a strong smell could mean only one thing: there was a *lot* of salt inside the cabin. He began to tremble with excitement.

The next moment Ereth rushed out from beneath the cabin, bounded through the snow drifts, scrambled up the front steps, made his way to the door, then thrust his black nose into the crack where the door met the frame. He inhaled deeply.

"Penguin peanuts," he whispered in awe. "There must be a ton of the stuff in there." His teeth chattered with anticipation.

Struggling to contain himself, Ereth examined

the door intently. When he realised it was padlocked, he began to shove it with his forehead as well as his front paws. It wouldn't budge.

Furious, he backed off and studied the walls of the cabin. About four feet off the ground – to the right of the door – was a small glass window. Perhaps he could get in that way.

Since Ereth climbed trees with ease, working his way up the side of the log cabin to the window ledge proved no problem. Once there he pressed his face to the glass pane and peered inside. A small table stood in one corner of the room. It was littered with plates, knives, and forks – even food. In the middle of the table stood a glass jar filled with salt.

"*Salt,*" Ereth murmured even as he began to drool. "A whole jar of salt." In a frenzy now, he began to butt his head against the window.

Ereth worked harder, certain that just a little more effort would shove it in entirely. "Pitted potwallopers!" he cried, as he thumped away. "Open up!"

Even as the window began to give, Ereth heard a voice from the woods behind him. "Help!" came the cry. "Someone help me! *Please!*"

"Mosquito mung," Ereth grunted angrily as he

tried to ignore the cry from the woods. Intent upon his task, he worked feverishly, poking his claws in and around the edges of the cabin window, trying to push it in. "Open up!" he shouted.

"Won't someone help me?" came yet another call.

"No, I won't!" Ereth replied out loud. "I've got better things to do."

Butting against the window as well as shoving with his paws, he gave a great grunt of exertion. The window fell in, striking the wood floor with the sound of shattering glass.

The smell of salt saturated the air. "Oh, my, oh, my," the porcupine crooned with excitement. "A room of salt! It's heaven. It's bliss."

"Help! I'm hurt," came the wail from the woods, more desperate than ever.

Prepared to leap down into the room, Ereth felt compelled to look back over his shoulder.

"I'm dying," came yet another cry. "Please. Help me."

"Donkey doughnuts," Ereth griped, glaring in the direction of the woods. "Why does everybody have to call on *me* for help? Used to be, taking care of yourself was what the world was about. It's not as if anybody cares about *my* life!" he added with exasperation.

"Please help!" came the cry again.

Ereth shook his head in frustration. "Buckled badger burgers!" he complained. "I'm never going to enjoy eating this salt with that racket in my ears." Angry and frustrated, Ereth crawled down from the window, tail first.

For a moment he stood at the edge of the porch and gazed furiously at the still falling snow. Every tree and bush was coated with thick white frosting. Branches were bent, small shrubs partially flattened. In the deepening dusk the whiteness seemed to be turning purple with cold.

"Maybe it's a trick," Ereth suddenly thought. "Maybe somebody wants to get me away so he can have the salt for himself. Or maybe . . ." it suddenly occurred to him, "somebody is trying to lure me into the woods."

Ereth considered that notion only briefly. "Anybody messing with me gets a quill up his snoot faster than a diving owl with lead claws."

With another look back at the cabin and a

deep sniff of the salt, Ereth waddled down the steps and plunged into the snow.

The snow had become deeper. To make any progress Ereth had to leap forward by fits and starts. Every few leaps he paused to catch his breath. But now that he had committed himself to finding the creature, the cries for help had ceased.

"I'll bet anything the dunce who was calling is better," Ereth muttered. He pushed on almost out of spite. "Catastrophic coyote culls! If it wasn't for this idiot I could be eating that salt right now. But no. Kind, old Ereth always puts others before himself. Blessed saint is what I am. Bursting bird bloomers!" he cried, lashing his tail about in anger. "I never think of myself. *Never!* Well, when I find whoever called I'll give him a piece of my mind – and tail – so he won't ever send out false alarms again." With such thoughts, Ereth plunged in among a cluster of trees.

Suddenly he stopped. Directly ahead, but hidden by a cornice of snow, he heard the sound of thrashing and clanking, followed by a soft whimpering. This was followed by a piteous *"Please."*

Whoever had been calling was not only still in trouble, it sounded as if he was growing weaker.

Ereth lifted his nose and sniffed. An animal was right in front of him. The question was, what kind? He couldn't tell because another smell filled the air. Though this second smell was familiar, Ereth could not quite grasp its nature. "Wilted wolf waffles," he muttered, "what is it?"

His frustration abetted by curiosity, Ereth took two more leaps forward in the snow, then stopped and gasped in horror.

7

Ereth Makes a Promise

On the ground lay a slim fox with tawny red fur and a long, bushy tail. The lower part of her delicate, pointed face and much of her muzzle were white. Her few remaining whiskers were as black as her nose. Black too was the outline of her almond-shaped, orange-coloured eyes. Her pointed ears were limp. All around her, the beaten-down snow was red with blood, for the fox's left front paw was gripped in the jaws of a steel spring trap.

In an instant Ereth understood: she had been caught in one of the traps that the hunters from the cabin had set.

The trap consisted of a pair of metal jaws, which — once sprung — had crushed the fox's paw, biting savagely through fur, flesh, muscles, and tendons. All were exposed. The amount of blood that lay about suggested the fox had been trapped for a long time. It was the blood that had confused Ereth's sense of smell.

Just to look upon the scene turned Ereth's bone marrow colder than the snow.

The fox, not yet realising anyone else was there, whimpered softly to herself as she tried to move her paw. Though extremely weak, she managed to lift the trap an inch or two. It was connected to a stake by a metal link chain. When the trap moved the chain jangled. Her effort — small as it was — was an enormous struggle, so much so that after a painful moment, she dropped paw, trap, and chain and lay panting with exhaustion.

As Ereth, horrified, continued to watch, the fox leaned forward and tried to gnaw at the chain, then at the trap itself.

"Murdering mud malls," Ereth growled under his breath.

His words were just loud enough for the fox to hear. Slowly, she turned her head.

Her nose was dry, caked with blood. Her whiskers were bent and broken. Her eyes were so glazed over with pain and tears, Ereth was not certain she grasped that he was there. "Can . . . can I . . . do anything?" he managed to say.

The fox cocked her head slightly, taking in the

words as if they came from a distant place. This time Ereth was sure she saw him. "I'm . . . caught . . ." she said in a weak voice. "Please help . . . me."

Ereth, fighting waves of nausea, drew closer. The smell of blood, the sight of the fox's mangled paw, were making him feeble. "I'm . . . awfully sorry," he whispered.

"Yes . . ." was all the fox could reply.

Gingerly stretching his head forward, Ereth attempted to bite the chain, the trap itself, and the spike which held the trap to the ground. Bitterly cold, iron hard, the metal would not give.

"How long have you been here?" he asked.

"All day."

"Mangled moose marbles," Ereth whispered with fright.

"It's been . . . so long," the fox said.

"I . . . see."

"The moment it happened I knew I would never get free," the fox went on. The snow, fluttering softly through the trees, clung to her fur like a delicate shroud. "I'm going to die," she said after a few moments. The words took a great deal of her energy to speak.

For once in his life Ereth did not know what to say. Though he wished there was something he could do, he had no idea what it might be.

"But — " the fox went on, gazing at Ereth with dark-rimmed eyes, "I want to ask you . . . to . . . promise me something."

"Of course," Ereth blurted with relief. "Whatever it is, I'll do it."

"You're . . . very kind," the fox whispered.

Ereth was about to ask her how she knew he was kind but decided against it.

"Not far from here . . . " the fox went on, speaking with increasing difficulty, "is my . . . den."

"Yes . . . "

"In the den are my . . . three cubs. They're only a few months old."

"Three cubs?" Ereth echoed, not grasping what the fox was leading to.

"Two sons, one daughter," the fox explained. "They don't know . . . what's happened to me. I went out in search of some fresh food for them when . . . I stepped on this . . . trap and . . . got caught."

"Salivating skunk spots," Ereth whispered. In spite of himself he looked anxiously about in search of other traps. How many had those humans said they set? Was it sixteen? Twenty?

"The snow hid it," the fox went on. "And . . . took away its smell."

Ereth licked his lips nervously.

"Would . . . you," the fox continued, "could you . . . be kind enough . . . to go to my cubs. They . . . need to be told what's become of me."

"I . . . suppose so," Ereth stammered, taken by surprise.

"They are very young. Helpless," the fox went on. "If you could just . . . take care of them . . ."

"Take care of them!" Ereth cried.

The fox blinked tears. "It would be so generous. Just knowing that you . . . would . . . I might . . . die with some measure . . . of peace."

"But . . . buttered flea foofaraws!" Ereth cried. "Where's . . . where's their father? Isn't he around?"

The fox turned away. "I don't know where he is," she said. "He's . . . gone off."

"Puckered peacocks," Ereth said indignantly. "That's not right. Or fair. I mean . . . it's absolutely un — "

The fox turned and gazed at Ereth with such

sorrowful eyes he shut his mouth and wished he had not spoken so loudly.

"Would you . . . please, *please*, promise you'll take care . . . of my cubs? Show them some . . . kindness? I love them so much. They're not old enough to take care of themselves . . . yet."

"But . . . oh, chipped cheese on monkey mould," Ereth growled, feeling sick to his stomach. "I suppose . . . I . . . could . . . for a bit. But only a bit," he added hastily.

"Thank you," the fox said. "They will be . . . so . . . appreciative. And so . . . will I. You are a saint to do so." The fox's eyes were closed now. Her breathing had become more difficult.

"Zippered horse zits," Ereth swore as he realised the fox was getting worse and worse.

"My den . . . is about . . ." the fox said, paying no mind to Ereth, ". . . a mile from here. Due east . . . in a low bluff. Behind . . . a pile of boulders. Just behind . . . a big blue rock."

"*Blue?*"

"A little . . . bit." The fox was fading rapidly.

"Low bluff . . . due east . . . blue rock," Ereth repeated.

"Thank you," the fox murmured, "thank you . . . so very much."

"I'll do it," Ereth sputtered. "But only for a short time, you understand. Only until their father gets back. I mean, I've no intention, none whatsoever, of taking the place of real parents who have the responsibility to – "

Ereth stopped speaking. It was obvious – even to him – that the fox had died.

For a long while Ereth stared at the dead fox. Twice he swallowed hard and sniffed deeply.

The smell of death filled the air. It frightened him deeply. "Jellied walrus warts," he mumbled as he hastened away from the scene.

For a while he went on silently, only to suddenly halt, lift his head, and bellow, "Dying! It's such a stupid way to live! It makes no sense at all!"

Taken aback by his own outburst, Ereth gave himself a hard, rattling shake. "It has nothing to do with me. *Nothing!*" he added savagely. "I'm going to live forever!"

He gazed up at the sky. It had stopped snowing. In the darkness a dull moon revealed rapidly moving shreds of clouds. It made the sky look like a torn flag. Stars began to appear, cold and distant. "Waste of time, stars," Ereth complained.

He went on, only to stumble into a ditch and sink up to his neck in snow. "Suffocating snow!" he screamed with fury. "Why does it have to be cold and wet?" With a furious snort he hauled himself up and shuddered violently.

Grudgingly, painfully, he recalled his promise to the fox, that he would help her three cubs. His heart sank. He groaned.

"Oh, why did I ever say I would do it?" he reproached himself. "I didn't mean it. I only said it to make her feel better. Fact is, I should have ignored her cries. I'm old enough to know better. Help someone and all you do is get into trouble. Always. I don't even like to be my own friend. But then I befriended Poppy. And accepted her husband. Then I was nice to their children. I should have kept to myself. Better to be alone. To stay alone.

"Helping others," he snarled viciously. "Being good! It's all broccoli bunk and tick toffee. Oh, pull the chain and throw up buckets! What am I going to do?"

8

Following and Moving On

Marty the pine marten had been as surprised as Ereth when the fox's call came out of the woods. He looked from Ereth to the woods, from the woods to Ereth, wondering what he should do.

Of course, Ereth had made the decision for him. When the porcupine broke away from the cabin and went lumbering through the snow toward the sound of the call, a puzzled Marty followed from a safe distance.

Then he saw Ereth disappear behind a mound of snow and heard low voices.

Alarmed, he swiftly, silently crawled up a tree and out along a branch, then looked down. When he saw the trapped fox, he was so startled he almost fell out of the tree.

As the fox and Ereth talked, Marty watched. He could not hear what they were saying. Then the fox slumped down, and the porcupine backed away. The next moment Ereth hurried off.

Staring at the scene below, Marty was filled with anger. The fox was dead. He knew who she was, too. Leaper. He knew of her cubs, and her husband. "Humans . . ." the pine marten hissed with fury. Then he saw where Ereth had gone, and his anger redoubled. "Look at him! He thinks he's beyond all that! Just runs off, the self-centred good-for-nothing . . . " More than ever, Marty resolved to catch the porcupine.

"I'm probably only going to get one chance," he reminded himself. "It has to be right. As long as he stays beneath the trees I'll be fine.

"Be patient Marty, be very patient," he told himself as he resumed his stalking.

Ereth plunged on through the thick, soft snow. "She said they were cubs," he mumbled to himself with disgust. "Three months old. Babies. Nothing but poop and puke, puke and poop. Helpless. Brainless. Useless. The only thing I hate more than children is babies. *Babies,*" he sneered with contempt. "Never could figure out why there are so many babies. They can't *do* anything . . .

"Right," he said, halting in his tracks. "And

that means I should forget the whole thing, head back to the salt, and for once, do something nice for myself!"

Then Ereth had a terrible thought. *The traps.* Hadn't the humans said they had staked out many of them? With so much snow the traps would be as invisible and odourless to him as they had been to the fox. They could be anywhere. He could be caught.

Engulfed by rising panic, he began to move forward again, but now each step he took was a cautious one.

Now and again he paused nervously to check over the trail he had made. It looked as if someone had dragged a bulky bag through the snow. "I could follow my own trail back," he told himself. "Safe once, safe twice." He turned around.

"Except . . ." he muttered, "I suppose *somebody* needs to tell those cubs what happened to their mother. If they come looking for her . . . they might get caught, too." The thought was too ghastly for Ereth to contemplate.

Besides — he told himself — if he did not tell the cubs what happened, they might never know. Being stupid youngsters, they were liable to just sit there and wait for her to come back. Doing nothing for themselves, they would starve to death. "That's the way the young are," Ereth thought, "always waiting for someone to give them a handout – even if the waiting kills them."

He turned back around and continued in the direction of the fox den.

"Of course," his thoughts continued, "if they did know what happened – I mean, if they had any brains, which isn't very likely – they could go out and find their father. That's what they should do. Let *him* take care of them.

"Wonder where the father is. Gone for a holiday, probably. Foxes are such idiots. But then, all meat eaters are idiots!"

Ereth groaned. "All that incredible salt sitting there and . . . I could use some sleep."

Once again he looked back in the direction of the log cabin. For a second he thought he saw what appeared to be a shadow moving high among the branches. It startled him.

"You're getting jumpy," he told himself. "No, not jumpy. Gilded carrot quoits," he swore. "The truth is, I don't want to do what I promised to do."

He rubbed his nose and sniffed. "Then again, I suppose it won't hurt me to drop by and tell those cubs what happened. The salt isn't going to walk away. And maybe I could sleep in their den – long as it does-n't stink of meat – then get back to the salt in the morning.

"Now where did she say those cubs were?" the porcupine wondered out loud as he peered around. "About a mile east from where I found her. In a low bluff. Behind some rocks. A blue rock. Oh, boiled badger boogers!" he growled in exasperation. "I hate this!"

He studied the scene before him. With every-thing buried in snow, it was hard to distinguish any-thing – rocks, boulders, bushes – much less determine where he was.

Coming out from the woods Ereth found an open field stretching before him. Blanketed in snow, it lay in perfect stillness. The new snow – untouched, untrod upon – appeared to have been there since time began. Moonlight gave it a radiant glow.

At the far end of the field was a bluff. It rose up sharply, as if half a hill had simply dropped away. Peering at it, Ereth could see the lumpy outline of rocks and boulders beneath the snow.

"Chipmunk tail squeezers," Ereth said. "I bet that's where her den is." It fitted the fox's description and seemed logical. Anyone approaching the den from across the field would be seen from a safe distance. And it wasn't likely anyone would drop down to the den from the top of the bluff. It was too steep.

"But how am I, in the middle of the night, supposed to find a blue boulder that's buried in the snow?"

With a snarl that was half anger, half weariness, Ereth moved out across the field. Suddenly he stopped. "Goat gaskins and maggot mange!" he cried. "What am I supposed to say to those cubs?" The thought of it made him groan out loud.

"Tell it to them straight," he told himself. "Right off. They'll have to face the mucus some time or other. It's a rough world. No sentimental slip-slop for me.

"I'll say: 'Hello! Guess what? Here's the news. Your mother's dead. Go find your father. Goodbye.'

"Yes. That's the way it's going to be. If they don't like it, they can eat my quills."

Grimly determined, Ereth continued to push forward. As he went he kept practicing his speech.

"Hello! Guess what? Here's the news. Your mother — "

It took him a while to reach the base of the bluff. Once there he halted and searched for some clue that might tell him where the fox's den was. But now that he was close he could see that there were *many* boulders embedded in the bluff. Every one was jagged and irregular. In the best of weather the den's entryway would be masked. Now it was further hidden by snow. "Lazy lizard lips," Ereth complained bitterly. "If those cubs are deep inside some den, I'll never find them!"

More weary than ever, the porcupine waddled along the base of the bluff in search of some meaningful sign.

Suddenly he heard a single yelp. It seemed to come from within the bluff itself. Ereth had no doubt it was one of the cubs. He was close. He held his breath in the hope that the sound would be repeated.

Though it took some time — Ereth was shivering by now — it came. This time the yelp was behind him. With a grunt of exasperation the old porcupine wheeled about, trying to determine the exact location of the sound. Once again there was only silence. "Bat bilge," the porcupine muttered angrily. "Since I'm spending so much time looking for them, the least they could be is helpful!"

He took another step and paused. From almost right over his head he heard an explosion of yelps.

He peered up the bluff to see a particularly jagged group of rocks. He began to move up. Upon reaching the first of the boulders he scratched the snow away to expose the surface. The rock was dark, but in the moonlight it had a blue cast.

Ereth had no doubt he was close to the den. But where was the entry?

He crawled higher. Twice he slipped back and had to struggle to keep himself from tumbling all the way to the bottom. The more he looked, the more exasperated he became. There didn't seem to be an entry. If there was one — and there had to be — it was so cleverly hidden he would never be able to find it.

Sighing deeply, Ereth wondered what he should do. He was exhausted. Angry. "Wet worm water," he whispered between chattering teeth. "Why did I ever agree to do this! Why did I ever leave home? Oh, Poppy, why did you abandon me?"

He took some deep breaths and shut his eyes. He had hardly done so when he felt a sharp smack on his nose.

9

Ereth Speaks

"Hello, Porky! You looking for someone?" yelped a high-pitched voice.

Ereth opened his eyes. A young female fox, head cocked to one side, was looking at him quizzically with bright, orange eyes. Her fur was fuzzy red, her muzzle white, her ears too large for her young head. Her front paws seemed oversized too, while the dark fur that covered them made it appear as if she were wearing baggy knee socks.

Ereth blinked. "Sparrow spittle," he sputtered. "What did you call me?"

"Porky," the fox said cheerfully. "Isn't that what you are, a porcupine?"

"My name is Erethizon Dorsatum," Ereth returned with hot dignity.

"Are you a male or female?"

"Male, needle nose!"

"My name isn't needle nose, it's Nimble," returned the fox. "And I'm a female."

"Do you live here?"

"Oh, sure," Nimble returned. "There's me and my brothers, Tumble and Flip. Then there's our mother. Her name is Leaper."

"Do you have a father?"

"Silly. Of course we do. His name is Bounder."

"I suppose that's him," Ereth muttered even as it was perfectly clear that he had found the fox's den and her three cubs.

"When we heard you coming," Nimble said, "we thought you were Mum."

"Why?"

"She's been away an awfully long time."

"Oh, right," Ereth said nervously.

"Bet you'll never guess what happened today?" Nimble said.

"What?"

"Some humans came by. They were walking around the field and the base of the bluff. Doing stuff. We don't know what."

"The trappers," Ereth thought with dread. "What did you do?" he asked.

"Nothing. Hid like Mum told us to do. Don't worry. They never saw us."

Ereth took a deep breath and said, "Guess what?"

"What?"

"Here's the news . . . " But Ereth could not go on. Tongue-tied, he could only mutter, "I'm not your mother."

"Oh, I know that," Nimble said, laughing. "I may be young, but I'm not stupid. You don't look like her at all. I mean, she's very beautiful. And, no offence, you're ugly. No way I'd confuse you with her. But have you seen her, by any chance? See, Mum went hunting this morning. To get us some fresh food. Like she always does. Only, like I said, she hasn't been back for a very long while. We think it was this white stuff."

"You mean . . . the snow?" Ereth asked.

"Oh. Is that what it's called? We never saw snow before."

"Why not?"

"Because we were born only a couple of months ago, silly."

"Lungfish loogies," Ereth said.

"What did you say?"

"I said, *lungfish loogies!*" Ereth barked.

Nimble cocked her head to one side. "Why did you say that?"

"Because I wanted to, bean head!"

The young fox stared open-mouthed at Ereth, trying to understand him. "Oh," she said with a sudden grin, "I get it. You're trying to be funny."

"Gallivanting glowworms!" Ereth roared. "I am not trying to being funny! I'm serious."

The next instant two more fox faces popped up behind Nimble and stared at Ereth. They looked very much like their sister, with red coats, white muzzles, ears much too big for their heads, and very large paws. Ereth could hardly tell them apart. When they looked at him, their faces showed disappointment.

"Who is that?" one of them asked Nimble.

"That, Flip, is a very funny old porcupine," Nimble replied. "His name is Earwig Doormat."

"It is not Earwig Doormat! It's Erethizon Dorsatum!"

Nimble grinned. "But *Doormat* is easier to say."

"He smells nasty," the other young fox whispered to Nimble. Ereth assumed it was Tumble.

"Has . . . has he seen Mum?" Flip asked.

"I asked him."

"What . . . what did he say?"

"He didn't."

"Mr Doormat," Flip asked shyly, "have you seen our mother?"

"Look here, brush tails," Ereth cried. "The name is Ereth, not Doormat, and I've been out in the snow all day and night. I'm cold. I'm wet. I'm hungry. Do you think you could show some manners and invite me into your den? Or don't foxes know how to be polite?"

"Of course we do," Nimble said brightly. "Mum taught us. I just didn't think you'd want to. Come on in and make yourself at home."

With that the three foxes whirled around and disappeared. Though it happened right before Ereth's eyes, he was not sure where they had gone.

"Where the frosted frog flip-flops are you?" he screamed.

Nimble stuck her head up from behind a boulder. "Right here, Doormat."

"Stop calling me 'Doormat'!" demanded Ereth as he lumbered up to where the young fox, a saucy look on her face, was waiting. "The name is Ereth."

"Perish?"

"Ereth!"

"Oh, okay," Nimble returned. "Whatever you say is fine with me. Just watch your step."

Ereth scrambled over a mound of snow, then poked his nose down into a hole. Out of it wafted a smell of rotting meat so strong he gagged.

"Are . . . are you coming?" Flip called.

Deciding he had no choice, Ereth yelled, "Of course I'm coming!"

The porcupine lumbered down a steeply sloped tunnel some six feet in length. At the bottom it opened up into a large, roomy area. It was warm but rank with the stench of old meat.

As Ereth came into the den, the three young cubs — lined up side by side — were sitting on their haunches, tongues lolling, heads cocked to one side, eyes bright and eager, staring at Ereth with curiosity.

Trying hard to recall who was who, the porcupine looked around.

In one corner, old leaves had been heaped together into a mound. Ereth assumed it was where the foxes slept. In another corner lay a small pile of gnawed bones. From the look of them Ereth guessed it was the remains of small animals, voles, mice, and the like: meals. Ereth, who hated even the thought of eating meat, felt revulsion.

Nimble said, "I'm sorry we can't offer you any food. We've eaten everything. That's why Mum went out."

"But she'll be back any minute," Tumble insisted in his sulky way.

"She doesn't usually stay away so long," Flip offered.

"Which is okay," Nimble added, "except we're pretty hungry. We think," she went on, "that with all this white stuff — it's called snow" — she explained to the others — "that covered everything, Mum probably had to go a long way. That's why she hasn't come back yet."

"What . . . what . . . do you think?" Flip asked Ereth in a quavering voice.

Ereth hardly knew what to say. Twice he opened his mouth and tried to deliver his prepared speech, only to have the words stick in his throat.

"Are you trying to say something?" Tumble demanded.

"I was going to say, 'Giraffe jelly.'"

The young foxes looked at one another in puzzlement.

"What?" Tumble asked.

"I said, 'Giraffe jelly'!" Ereth shouted.

For a moment no one said a thing. Then Tumble demanded, "Mr Perish, how come you're here?"

"The name," the porcupine yelled, "is Ereth! As for why I'm here . . . Well, I . . . I like taking walks. That's why."

"In all that . . . snow?" Flip cried.

"Do you have a problem with that, dribble-nose?"

The foxes looked at one another again. Nimble giggled. Flip grinned shyly. Even Tumble – though he seemed more reserved and serious than the other two – smiled.

"I suppose not," Flip replied.

Ereth shifted uncomfortably on his feet. "Look here," he began, trying to find the courage to speak the truth. "I've got something to say to you. Something . . . really important."

"Oh, that's nice," Nimble said. "We'd really like to hear it. What is it?"

"It's . . . it's . . . Oh, sugared snail spit . . . I . . . spoke to your mother."

"You did! Where is she? Why hasn't she come home?" the cubs cried out.

"She . . . she . . . won't be coming home," Ereth blurted out.

The young foxes stared at him in bewilderment.

Ereth swallowed hard. "And that's . . . because . . ."

"Because of *what?*" Tumble asked sharply.

"Great gopher underpants!" Ereth cried out. "What makes you think I know?"

"Because you just said you did," Nimble pointed out.

"Moth milk." Ereth sighed. He stared at the cubs. They were gazing at him with rapt attention. Nimble had her mouth open, panting gently. There were lines of anger over Tumble's eyes. Flip's eyes were full of tears.

The emotion was too much for Ereth. "Sour snake sauce on spaghetti!" he suddenly cried. "Forget it!" Whirling around, he scrambled for the entry tunnel.

"Mr Perish Doormat," Flip called after him, "did . . . did something happen to Mum?"

Ereth stopped in his tracks. Slowly, he turned back to face the young foxes.

"We . . . need to know," Flip said.

"No, you don't!" Ereth snapped.

"We do too!" Tumble insisted.

"No!"

"But why?"

"Because," Ereth shouted with complete exasperation, "Oh, fish feather fruitcakes . . . because your mother is dead, that's why!"

10
Ereth and the Cubs

The three young foxes gazed at Ereth with eyes full of disbelief. No one spoke.

It was Flip who finally stammered, "Would . . . would you repeat that?"

"Sorry," Ereth grumbled. "I . . . ah . . . didn't mean to say it that way." Flustered, wishing he could be anywhere else in the world but where he was, he backed up a step. "And I wouldn't have either if . . . you hadn't made me. I mean, I'm . . . sorry. I am . . ." His voice faded away.

"But," Flip asked in a quavering cry, "did you say that Mum . . . died?"

"Yes."

"How . . . how do you know?"

"It had nothing to do with me," Ereth said. "I was an innocent bystander."

"Died?" Nimble echoed, her voice rising tremulously.

"I said yes, didn't I?"

"But how's that possible?" Tumble wailed. "Mums . . . can't die. They're supposed to take care of us. *Always.*"

Ereth swallowed hard. "There is this cabin. With salt. And it's my birthday. Except that has nothing to do with it. Only, because I was there, I heard her. She . . . stepped into a trap. And . . . she . . . couldn't get out. She bled . . . badly . . . too much."

"Did . . . did you speak to her?" Flip asked. "Before she . . . died?"

"Yes."

"What did she say?" Nimble asked.

"Look here," Ereth sputtered. "I never had to . . . do this before. Never wanted to. And I . . . oh, spread peanut butter on pink poodle!" he screamed. "I don't know what to say!"

"I don't care what *you* have to say," Tumble barked angrily. "Just tell us what *she* said!"

"Oh, right," Ereth muttered. "She . . . said a . . . lot of things. Mostly . . . sentimental slip-slop. No! I didn't mean that. I mean, well, she said you were helpless. That you couldn't take care of yourselves. Wanted me to find you and tell you . . . what happened. Asked me to take care of you. It was all . . . well, ridic — I mean, sad. And I suppose I will stay . . . but only until your father comes home. Understand that? Only till then. That's what she said."

"Nothing . . . else?" Flip asked after a moment.

"Well . . . she also said . . . she . . ." — Ereth almost choked on the word — "loved . . . you."

Nimble stared at Ereth dumbly. Tumble, tail between his legs, backed away. Flip's eyes filled with tears.

Ereth turned away and shuffled into a corner. Hearing nothing from the trio, he looked back over his shoulder. The young foxes were gazing after him as if they could not believe what had been said.

Then Flip slowly lifted his head, squeezed his eyes shut, opened his mouth, and let forth an earsplitting, dismal yowl that saturated the den with its misery. The two other foxes did the same until all three were howling together. Howl after howl they cried, filling the den with their anguish. On and on they went, with such a volume that Ereth, becoming fearful that he would lose his mind, spun about and shouted, "Stop it! Stop it at once!"

As if a switch had been flicked, the foxes ceased their cries and just sat and sniffled.

"Food!" Ereth cried in desperation. "You have to eat food."

The foxes looked at him blankly.

He said, "You said you hadn't eaten all day."

"That was because Mum . . ." Nimble stopped in midsentence.

"Right," Ereth snapped. "She went out to get you some. Now, just tell me, what do you eat?"

Tumble shrugged. "Whatever she brought us. Chipmunks, moles, and voles. Rabbits if she was lucky. Mice, too. They're great appetizers. But then I'm very particular about what I eat."

Ereth grimaced. "I *hate* meat eaters," he said.

"Well, we love meat," Tumble threw back defiantly. "It's what Mum always gave us."

"Don't you eat anything else?"

"Bugs," Tumble snapped.

"Oh, green goose cheese!" Ereth cried with disgust. "How about some decent food? Like . . . like vegetables."

Nimble wrinkled her nose. "Only if we have to. You know, berries and stuff. No offence, but we like meat much better."

"In fact," Tumble said, "we hate vegetables."

"Yeah," Flip agreed. "They're really nasty."

Ereth studied the faces of the young foxes. They were looking at him as if he knew what to do, as if he had answers. "Do you do any hunting for yourselves?" he asked.

"I . . . I caught a grasshopper once," Flip said with pride. "It was crunchy."

Ereth almost threw up.

"Did your mother hide any food?" he asked. "Foxes do that, you know."

"They do?" Nimble said. She turned to her brothers with a questioning look. They seemed equally surprised.

"'Course they do," Ereth snarled. "Everybody knows that. She probably had another den, too. Or more. A just-in-case den. Am I right?"

"Oh, that," Nimble replied. "It's down along the bluff a bit. Not too far from here."

"Would there be any food there?"

Nimble shrugged. "Mum only told us what we needed to know."

"Can you find it?"

The foxes exchanged glances again. "Yes . . . I suppose. Maybe."

"Then why the mangy muskrat mites, if you were so hungry, didn't you go there to look for food?"

There was a moment of embarrassed silence. "I suppose we didn't think," Flip offered after a moment.

"We were waiting for Mum," Tumble said belligerently. "The way she told us to."

"And we always do what she tells us," Nimble explained more softly.

"Anyway, the . . . white stuff came," Flip added.

"Snow," Nimble reminded him.

Ereth said, "I suppose we'd better check that place. Now you, Nimble, take the lead. You seem to know where this place is. Then Tumble, Flip, you follow. I'll come behind. Come on, let's hit it."

For a moment the foxes just looked at him.

It was Flip who said, "Mr Doormat are . . . are you going to be our mother from now on?"

"Look here, you simple smear of wallaby wax," Ereth roared, "the name is *Ereth*, not Doormat. Secondly, I am not your mother. I can't be a mother. I don't want to be a mother. I'm only taking care of you until – " Ereth stopped.

"Until what?" Tumble prompted quickly.

"Until . . . your father gets back. Which had better be as fast as bees buzzing buttercups. Do you understand?"

The foxes stared at him.

Exasperated, Ereth asked, "Do you have any idea where he is?"

"He happens to be doing his business!" Tumble returned hotly. "He's got a lot of it."

"Sorry I asked," Ereth returned in the same tone. "Just hop it! To the other place."

The three foxes, energised by Ereth's yelling, tumbled out of the den. The weary porcupine followed, close enough to hear Tumble whisper to the others, "Wow, he's a nasty one, isn't he?"

II
Marty the Pine Marten

In the field below the bluff sat Marty the pine marten, up to his neck in snow. The skies had cleared. The moon was full. The air was still. Not a sound could be heard. The world glowed with a serene whiteness.

Not that Marty the pine marten cared or even noticed any of that. He was angry at himself for allowing Ereth to get away. His strategy, once he realised that the porcupine was heading toward the far side of the field, was to trap the prickly creature against the wall of earth. He was quite sure this would work. But to Marty's great puzzlement, Ereth had simply vanished. It was as if he had been swallowed up by the bluff itself.

"Perhaps," he thought, "he found an old badger's den. Or a cave. Maybe he's holing up till morning. Sleeping.

"Should I wait?" he asked himself. "Should I come back tomorrow? Should I forget all about this annoying Ereth? How irritating that he should get away from me!

"No," Marty decided. "I'll wait a bit. Until the moon's shadow goes from over there to over here."

He was still studying the scene when he saw three young foxes burst out of the bluff, followed momentarily by the porcupine.

"Not good," Marty said to himself with a frown. "I can deal with the porcupine, but not if those foxes are with him. They look young, but the four of them together will be too much to handle."

Even so, Marty told himself to be patient. "Porcupines and foxes do not mix," he reminded himself. "Sooner or later Ereth will be alone again." From a safe distance Marty watched to see where the quartet was going.

12
The Other Den

It was Nimble who led the way to the other den. Tumble and Flip followed on her heels. Last to come was Ereth. He could see right away why the foxes had been named the way they were. Each one of them moved through the snow in short, frolicking jumps. So energetic were they, they sometimes landed on one another's backs, or collided. Ereth, who could do nothing but plod stolidly after them, kept crying, "Slow down. Wait for me!" He was terribly nervous. What if one of the cubs put a foot into a trap? What if *he* did?

But whenever the weary Ereth caught up to them the cubs were off again, leaving the porcupine to mumble disparaging remarks about foxes and the world in general.

Though the second den was only some twenty yards from the one he had first entered, Ereth never would have found it on his own. In fact, when he finally caught up with the cubs they were hastily scraping back the snow from between two large boulders. Only when the snow was removed was a small hole revealed — smaller than the one that led into the other den.

"Is this it?" Ereth demanded, panting from exertion.

"It's what we told you about," Flip assured him.

"Are there others?" Ereth asked, eyeing the narrow entryway.

"Don't know," Tumble said. Without another word, he scurried down the hole. Nimble followed.

"Are . . . are you coming?" Flip asked.

"I'll try," Ereth replied.

"I'd like you to," the young fox said shyly before he darted down the hole.

"Monkey middles," Ereth grumbled, as he braced himself to follow.

No sooner was he inside the tunnel than he felt himself squeezed from all sides. Grunting and groaning, scraping and pushing at the dirt, he found it hard to breathe.

"Are you still coming?" he heard one of the foxes call.

"Of course I am!" Ereth shouted.

"Hurry up. There's food down here!"

Ereth continued to kick and pull, gradually working his way forward. Suddenly Flip appeared in his face.

"Need some help?" he asked.

"Buzz off, you bowl of donkey droppings!" he cried. "I never need help! Never!"

"Sorry," Flip said quickly and retreated, leaving Ereth to struggle.

Twenty minutes later the exhausted porcupine squeezed into the den, bringing with him a shower of pebbles and dirt.

The three foxes were on their bellies, holding bones in their paws and gnawing at them.

Nimble looked up. "What took you so long?" she asked.

Ereth only said, "Did you find something to eat?"

"A lot," Tumble enthused, with his mouth full. "A really great half-eaten rabbit."

"Would . . . would you like some?" Flip offered.

"No!" roared Ereth. Though famished, he could only think about sleep.

He looked around the new den. Slightly smaller than the first, it was the same messy, nasty-smelling kind of place.

Without a word, the porcupine moved as far from the foxes as possible, then lay down. "I'm going to sleep," he announced. "And I just want you to know, this is the worst birthday of my life."

"What's a birthday?" Flip asked his sister in a low voice.

"It's the day you're born," Nimble explained.

"Oh, wow! Does that mean that Doormat was just born today?"

"No way," Tumble said. "He's got to be ancient."

Ereth closed his eyes, curled up, and tried to act as if he were already asleep.

"Really? How old do you think he is?" Flip asked in a whisper.

"From the way he's acting," Tumble asserted with great authority, "I'd say two hundred years, at least."

"Does that mean he'll die soon?"

"Probably."

"Shut up!" Ereth screamed.

For a moment there was silence.

"Sir," Flip said in a small voice. "Mr Perish?"

Ereth sighed. "I'm sleeping," he said.

"Oh."

A few quiet moments passed. Just as Ereth felt himself drifting off, he felt a nudge. He opened his eyes. The three foxes were standing next to him.

"What is it?" Ereth asked numbly.

Nimble said, "Mr Earwig, when we sleep at night, Mum lets us snuggle up close to her. She even wraps her tail about us. It keeps us very warm."

"Chewed over cow cuds," Ereth mumbled. "Will this day never end?"

"What should we do?" Tumble asked.

"Have you even looked at my tail?" Ereth snapped.

"What about it?"

"It's full of quills."

"Are you *completely* covered with quills?" Flip asked.

Ereth hesitated. "No," he admitted.

"Where aren't you?" Tumble demanded.

"My belly."

"Can we snuggle *there*?" Nimble asked.

"No!" Ereth roared.

"But we can't sleep," Tumble said after a moment. "Our mother . . ."

"I am not your mother!" Ereth shouted, turning his back to the foxes. "I'm a porcupine who wants to be left alone! Beat it!"

The foxes stared at him for a while. Then Flip turned and, with head bent low, trotted off to the farthest side of the den. Sighing, he flung himself down with his back to Ereth and curled up in a ball.

After a moment the other two followed their brother. In moments they were rolled up together like a flower bud.

Despite his exhaustion Ereth could not sleep. He kept thinking of all that had happened that day. "So help me," he muttered, "this'll be the last birthday I ever celebrate."

He began to drift off, only to hear a sound: a long, sad sigh. He tried to ignore it, but more sighs followed. The foxes were whimpering.

"Barbecued bear beards," Ereth swore to himself. Heaving himself up, he waddled over to where the foxes lay.

"Move over, you piebald pooper snoopers!"

He flung himself down and tried to flatten his

quills as much as possible. Then he rolled over, expos-
ing his soft, plump belly. Within moments he could
feel first Flip, then Nimble, and, after a pause, Tumble
push up against him, uttering sleepy sighs of comfort.

As he lay there the old porcupine's mind drifted to visions of his own snug, private log. He thought
of Poppy and Rye's children. Those children were a
nuisance too, constantly talking, asking him needless
questions. "But," he thought wistfully, "I never had to
be in charge of them. And at the end of the day they
always went away."

"Baked birthday boozers," Ereth managed to
say before he succumbed to deep and needed sleep.
"I'm trapped. Completely, utterly, miserably trapped."

13
Marty the Pine Marten

The morning dawned as bright as ice. New snow lay thick, softening everything jagged, even as it absorbed almost every noise. In all the landscape the only sound to be heard was the trilling of a tiny robin flitting among the tree branches along the edges of Dimwood Forest.

That small sound was enough to wake Marty the pine marten from his sleep. He had gone to bed beneath a pile of old leaves he'd found heaped against a rock by the forest rim. Before burrowing in and falling asleep, he'd vowed to wake as early as possible, promising himself that on the morrow he would catch that very annoying Ereth.

In fact the pine marten was more determined than ever to catch the old porcupine. He was not going to give up now.

When Marty had last seen Ereth – beneath the light of a midnight moon – the porcupine had been moving clumsily along the bluff in the wake of three tumbling young foxes. Even as Marty watched, the whole group had suddenly disappeared — into a den, or so the pine marten presumed.

Afterwards, Marty spent a good amount of time trying to guess why Ereth was with the foxes in the first place. He decided it must have something to do with Leaper.

Quickly throwing off remnants of sleepiness, Marty crept silently along the forest fringe. When he saw an aspen tree with a thick branch that stretched over the open field, he climbed it, then moved along the branch as far as he could safely go. From this high vantage point he had a complete view of the field — and that included the bluff.

"Be patient . . . " Marty urged himself yet again. "Be *very* patient. Ereth is doomed."

14
The Cubs

Deep within the fox den it was not noise that aroused Ereth from his fitful sleep, but immense aggravation. "Snake-smell soup," the porcupine protested as he recollected the appalling situation in which he'd placed himself.

Then he sensed his hunger. It seemed like forever since he'd eaten a decent meal. He had to get up. But when he made an attempt to move his cramped legs he only bumped into the three young foxes.

Slowly, not wanting to wake them, Ereth eased himself away from the leggy hugs of the cubs. Once free, he shook himself all over – producing a soft rattling sound – then turned to look at the sleeping youngsters.

"Wanting me to be their mother!" Ereth shook his head violently. "Rabbit earwax! What I need to do is get out of here before they get up."

Then and there Ereth made up his mind to head back to the log cabin before the trappers returned, have himself a feast of salt worthy of his efforts, then continue on. These cubs could take care of themselves.

Moving as noiselessly as he was able, Ereth crept to the entryway. When he reached it he paused. Recalling how difficult it had been to get through when he came down into the den, he eyed the hole anxiously. But no sooner did he brace himself to go forward than a twinge of guilt held him back.

Murmuring "Phooey on being decent," he turned to take one final look at the cubs – just to make sure they were sleeping. To his surprise, Nimble had raised her head and was staring at him with sleepy eyes.

"Mr Earwig, sir," Nimble asked with a yawn, "are you going out?"

An indecisive Ereth stood by the entryway. The only response he could come up with was, "The name, banana brain, is Ereth."

"Oh, right. I forgot. But, Ereth, *are* you going out?" Nimble asked again.

Ereth made a noncommittal grunt.

"I mean," the young fox inquired, "will you be coming back?"

"'Course I will," Ereth said gruffly. "Do you think I'd just abandon you?"

"I was only asking," Nimble said with a friendly wag of her tail. She yawned, revealing white teeth, red tongue, and gullet.

Ereth said, "I was just thinking about . . . food."

Nimble got up on all fours, stretched, and gave herself a shiver to loosen her stiff muscles. "Mr Perish . . . I mean, Ereth . . . I think you're too fat for the entryway. Would you like me to make it bigger? I'm pretty good at digging. That way you could come and go much more easily. You know, when you get us food."

Ereth grimaced but said nothing.

The young fox trotted up to the tunnel and made her way up to the ground surface. Within moments Ereth could hear her scratching and digging furiously. Gradually, she worked her way back down. When she emerged her face and fur were covered with dirt.

"There!" she offered with a grin. "It's a whole lot wider now."

"Thanks," Ereth grumbled as he moved toward

the entryway. Pushing and shoving, he got through the tunnel with somewhat less difficulty than the night before.

Outside, the dazzling whiteness of snow, the cloudless sky, and the golden sun made him blink. The field before the bluff lay smooth and undisturbed. And at the far side of the field was the edge of Dimwood Forest.

Though Ereth looked at the forest trees longingly – and dreamed of the tender under-bark that he knew was there for the eating – he worried about the cubs. "Where the blazing baboon balloons can I find them some food?" he asked himself with exasperation.

As he fretted, Nimble came out of the hole and sat beside him.

"Ereth, do you like snow?"

"No."

The young fox thought about this, and then said, "Do you like anything?"

"Salt."

After another interval, the fox asked, "Ereth . . ."

"What?"

"I may be wrong, but I don't think you want to stay with us."

Ereth made a noncommittal grunt.

"You know, it'll be fine with us if you leave. I mean, I don't think we need you."

Ereth said, "You're wrong."

"Why?"

"Because," Ereth said, "youngsters don't do well alone. You're takers, not givers. If there's no one to take from, you'll die."

"Oh, okay," Nimble said agreeably.

"Look here, elephant ears," Ereth suddenly barked, "I'm a vegetarian. I don't eat meat. I hate it. Just the thought of eating it makes me ill. So I don't have the slightest idea how to go about getting the kind of food you want."

"Mum used to go out into this field and listen."

"Listen?"

"Oh, sure. She could hear the most amazing things. I mean, pretty much anything that moved. She was wonderful. There were crunchy voles and tasty mice —"

"Stop!" Ereth snapped.

Nimble turned. "What's the matter?"

"No mice!"

"Are they bad for you?"

"Eat a mouse and you've had it," Ereth snarled. "Worst food in the world for foxes. Or anyone else for that matter. One hundred per cent poison."

"Thank you. I didn't know that."

Side by side, the two stared at the snow-covered field.

Then Nimble suddenly whispered, "Ereth! There's something moving right down there."

"Where?"

"In the snow," Nimble said. "At the bottom of the bluff. I'm pretty sure I can hear it." She dropped into a crouch, belly low to the ground.

"It would be a lot better if you ate bark," Ereth muttered.

Nimble was not listening. Ready to pounce, she began to move forward.

"I don't want to watch," Ereth said, feeling ill. With that he turned around and crept back down into the den.

The other two foxes had woken up.

"Where's Nimble?" Tumble demanded right away.

"Outside. Getting food."

"Why didn't you tell me?" groused Tumble, who bounded up the tunnel, leaving Ereth alone with Flip.

"Don't you want to hunt for food too?" Ereth asked him.

"I don't feel well."

"What's the matter?"

"I . . . I have a stomachache," the fox said.

"Galloping goat giggles," Ereth sneered. "*Why* do you have a stomachache?"

"I just do."

"Well, that's your problem, mustard mould. I have no idea what to do about it."

"Can I come lie near you?" Flip asked.

"Do whatever you want."

Flip came over to where Ereth was and stretched out, chin resting on his forepaws, large ears tilted forward, big eyes staring up at the porcupine.

Feeling uncomfortable under the gaze, Ereth shifted slightly.

"Mr Ereth . . . " Flip said.

"What?"

"I'm . . . glad it was you who brought us the news about . . . Mum."

"Oh, well, sure . . . fine," Ereth replied gruffly.

Neither fox nor porcupine spoke for a while.

Flip sighed. "I worked out something," he said.

"Yeah? What?"

"You don't like us very much."

"I do like you," Ereth growled.

"Do you like us enough to stay with us?"

"I told you I'd stay, didn't I? But the minute your father gets back, I'm out of here."

"Oh." Flip wiggled a little closer to Ereth. "Mr Ereth," he said, "I like you."

Ereth grunted. "Why?"

"You're nice, but I don't think you like it when I say that."

"Shut up!" Ereth snapped.

Tumble popped down from the entryway. "Ereth!" he cried.

"What?"

"Nimble couldn't catch that vole. So we're really hungry. It's your job to get us some food."

15
Chores

The three foxes sat side by side, tails wagging, tongues lolling, big eyes staring at Ereth.

"All right," the porcupine said. "It's perfectly obvious to anybody but a belching boomerang that there's a lot to get done. That means you've got work to do."

"Work?" Tumble asked, irritation in his voice. "What are you talking about?"

"Maybe you haven't noticed, sludge foot," Ereth snapped, "but there's a need to collect food, and to clean the mess around here. Look at those bones scattered about. And the floor! Messy! We need to get the meat stink out. I can't stand it. There's your sleeping pile too. It needs to be made neat. Just because you hung around me last night doesn't mean that it's going to happen again. From now on — as long as I'm around — you'll sleep on your side of the den, in your own bed. Am I making myself understood?"

The foxes stared at him blankly.

"All right then, who does what? What chores do you each have?"

The foxes exchanged puzzled looks.

"What's the problem?" Ereth demanded. "All I'm asking is, who does what around here?"

"We don't do any of that stuff," Tumble said disdainfully.

"Moose midges on frog fudge!" Ereth barked. "All I'm asking is, who does what chores?"

Flip said, "Mr Ereth, all we do is play. And eat."

"And sleep late," Nimble added.

"Then who the puppy pancakes does all the work around here?" Ereth demanded.

"Mum," Nimble replied.

"Right," Tumble said angrily. "So if you're going to be our mother, you should be doing all that stuff too."

"I am not your mother!" Ereth roared. "If you think I'm going to take care of you like some servant while you do nothing, you can go take a slide on the sludge pile.

"This is your den, not mine," he raged on. "And it's absolutely disgusting. So first of all, you're going to clean up."

"But I hate work," Tumble announced. "It gives me a headache."

"Look here, stinkweed," Ereth said. "You hankering to turn your nose into a pin cushion?"

"No."

"Then you'll work like everyone else."

Tumble glowered but said nothing more.

Ereth said, "Who's the best hunter?"

"I am," Nimble piped up. "I almost caught that vole. Next time I'm sure I'll get something."

"Fine, after we do the den you can go hunting. As for you," Ereth said to Tumble, "you'll keep the den floor clean. And you," he told Flip, "will make sure the bed is kept neat. Now hit it!" the porcupine roared.

The foxes didn't move.

"What's the matter?" Ereth demanded.

"What chores are *you* going to do?" Tumble asked.

"Look here," Ereth roared, "you wasted wedge of woodpecker wallow, this is your den, not mine!"

"But Mr Ereth sir," Flip asked cautiously, "don't you clean up your own den?"

"One more word out of any of you, and you'll get fifteen quills in each of your backsides." Ereth waved his tail ominously. "Now move it!"

With much sighing and grumbling as well as dirty looks at Ereth, the foxes set about their tasks.

Flip began by pushing the bed leaves into a pile, then went about the den picking up stray bits of leaves and twigs with his teeth and depositing them on the heap. Nimble, meanwhile, gathered gnawed bones and carried them one by one — and slowly at that — out of the nest, where she deposited them a short distance from the den's entryway. As for Tumble, he set about trying to smooth down the dirt floor of the den with his tail. In fact, he spent most of the time cleaning his tail of any twigs, leaves, and bone bits he happened to pick up.

A glowering Ereth watched the work progress. Now and again he called out useful suggestions, such as, "You missed that bone over there, sack foot!" Or, "Hey, armpit brain, don't forget to smooth down that corner."

The three foxes worked slowly, resting more often than they laboured. They also spent a considerable amount of time complaining about what they were doing. Then, whenever they got close to one another, they fell into bickering and snapping. More than once Ereth had to come between them.

"Mr Ereth?" It was Flip who called.

"What is it?" Ereth growled.

"Could you help me? I can't get the leaf pile right."

"What's the matter with it?"

"It's all lopsided. I need you to tell me what to do. Please."

With a grunt Ereth heaved himself up and waddled over to the corner where Flip was working. Balefully he surveyed the pile of leaves. It was as the fox had said. The leaves had simply been shoved into a corner where they were still quite a mess.

"Typical," Ereth muttered. "Youngsters don't know how to do anything right." In a fury of frustration the porcupine pushed the leaves from first one side, then another, shaping the mass into an orderly pile. As he worked Flip looked on approvingly, but did not lend a paw.

"There!" Ereth said, when he had finished. "Did you see how I did it?"

"Oh, wow!" Flip cried. "It looks so much better than I ever could have done. And you did it faster too."

Tail wagging with pleasure, he waded clumsily

into the pile, then threw himself down right in the middle. "Oh, this *is* wonderful," he barked with delight as he squirmed down so that the leaves were all about him. "You do it so well. You should do this chore all the time."

Flip lifted his head. "Hey, guys," he cried. "Look what nice Mr Ereth did to our bed."

As soon as Nimble and Tumble saw how cosily Flip had settled himself, they dashed over and leaped, paws first, into the pile.

As Ereth looked on in dismay, the three foxes began to tumble joyfully, wrestling, snarling, and snapping at one another until the entire leaf pile that Ereth had shaped had become a complete mess. With leaves scattered everywhere, the den was worse than it had been before.

"Stop!" Ereth cried. "Stop!"

The cubs, however, paid not the slightest attention to him, but continued their romp. A disgusted Ereth turned his back on them and went outside.

"Impossible," he kept saying to himself. "Completely, totally impossible. I can't do it. I just can't. I've been with them only one day, but if this keeps up, I'll be dead in a week."

16
Hunting

Ereth was staring glumly over the snowy field, trying to decide what to do next, when Nimble popped out of the hole.

"I'm ready," she announced brightly.

"Ready for what?"

"Don't you remember? You said hunting was to be my job."

"Is the den cleaned up?"

"It certainly is," Nimble assured him. "Do you want to see?"

"No."

"Okay. But if you want to teach me how to hunt, I'm ready to do it now."

"Antelope uncles!" Ereth swore. "I told you, I don't know anything about hunting."

"I should be a good hunter," Nimble said. "My mother was. And my father's really, really great."

Ereth looked around. "You have any idea when this father of yours is coming back?"

"Nope," Nimble said earnestly. "He just comes and goes. He's a very busy fox."

"Busy at what?"

Nimble's eyes narrowed. "Are you suggesting he isn't busy?"

Ereth decided not to pursue the matter. Instead he asked, "Where do you usually hunt?"

"Right down along the bluff here. Mum always said we mustn't go too far. Should I go then?" Nimble asked.

Ereth was about to say yes, when he thought about the human hunters' traps. "I'd better go with you," he announced.

"Great!" Nimble bounded off.

"Don't go so fast!" Ereth shouted after the fox, as his short legs struggled to carry him through the snow, over the rocks, and around the boulders.

Pausing, Nimble looked around and grinned to see how awkward Ereth was.

After much panting and scowling, Ereth caught up with the young fox. "Listen here, flea brain, your legs are a lot longer than mine. So keep it down to a decent crawl."

"I will. But — " She stopped speaking suddenly.

"What is it?" Ereth asked.

"I smell something."

"What? Where?"

"Right down there at the bottom," Nimble whispered.

Ereth looked, but could see nothing.

The young fox made her way down the face of the bluff, pointing her nose now this way, now that, sniffing.

Suddenly she froze. With her belly low to the ground, she stretched out to her full length.

"Be careful!" Ereth cautioned.

"Shhh!" Nimble replied. Tail stiff behind her, the young fox moved one step at a time, all but slithering towards whatever it was she had detected.

Ereth, trying to keep his eye on the cub but feeling more clumsy than ever, struggled hard to catch up, skidding and slipping over the rough terrain.

Below, Nimble prepared to pounce.

Suddenly, Ereth broke through the snow, only to strike a patch of rocks and boulders. His legs went out from beneath him. As he tried to right himself he caused a small landslide. Rocks and snow cascaded past the fox. One rock popped up into the air. It came down in front of Nimble's nose.

No sooner did the stone hit the snow than two jaws of steel rose up and snapped together, clamping on the rock with a horrifying metallic *clack!*

"Don't move!" Ereth screamed.

A baffled Nimble came up out of her crouch and stared at the object. "What . . . what is it?" she asked.

Ereth, heart hammering, shouted, "It's a trap! Don't breathe! Don't think!"

Nimble leaned forward and sniffed.

"Didn't you hear me, you broken bottle of chicken clots? There may be other traps near you." Moving with great caution, Ereth inched toward the exposed trap, his small black eyes looking this way and that.

"But . . . what's a trap?" Nimble asked.

"It's . . . made . . . by humans," Ereth said, struggling to get his breath back. "To catch . . . animals like you and me. It's what caught your mother. That's what killed her."

Nimble's eyes grew very big. "Oh," she said.

Ereth leaned forward toward the sprung trap. It had a hard, oily reek that turned his stomach. When he thought of their walk last night from one den to the other — and Nimble's pursuit of a vole — it made him feel faint to realise how lucky they had been.

Nimble came forward and sniffed at the trap again. "But . . . but it smells like good food," she said, still baffled.

"That's the bait," Ereth said. "And there are fourteen more of them."

"Oh, dear," Nimble said. In a small voice she said, "Where?"

"That's just the point, pig pill! I don't know!" Ereth was so upset he was shouting.

"But . . . why are you so angry at *me?*" Nimble asked, backing away.

"I am not angry at you!" Ereth screamed. "I'm angry at the whole world!"

"But . . . does that mean we can't go . . . anywhere?"

"It means we have to be super careful. The snow makes everything worse. You can't see anything. You'll have to think! Get it? For once in your life you're going to have to use your brindled bit of baby brain."

"I'm not a baby!"

"You're a child!" Ereth raged on. "It's the same thing. And I'm the one who has to take care of you!"

"No, you don't."

"No? If I hadn't thrown that rock right there, you would have never seen that trap."

"You didn't throw it, you fell, and it rolled down," Nimble pointed out. "It was nothing but stupid luck."

"Never mind luck! There are other traps around. Waiting to grab you. I can't rest easy until we get them all."

"But . . . but how do we do that?"

"That's the point, elbow ears!" Ereth screeched in frustration. "I don't know!" He turned away to hide the angry tears in his eyes. "All I know is that I have to do something. Fast!"

17
Traps

Ereth and the three cubs were sitting outside, next to the entryway to the den.

"Look here, fur balls," Ereth said to them. "I know you're impatient to get about. But as Nimble here can tell you, you can't just bop around like a bunch of giggling glitz glumpers. Tell them what happened."

Nimble looked around sheepishly. "I was just about to pounce – I think it was a mole I was smelling – when Ereth here kicked a rock. And this thing – "

"A trap," Ereth corrected.

"A trap sprang up right out of the snow. It's . . . really nasty. Ereth says it was the same kind of trap that . . . got Mum."

Tumble and Flip, having listened in silence, turned and stared where Nimble indicated.

"Remember the day of the snowstorm? And those hunters who were around? They put down sixteen of these traps," Ereth explained. "They could be anywhere, from the bluff right back into the forest and up to that cabin of theirs. No telling where they might be."

The cubs remained silent. Then Tumble said, "I'm hungry. You should be feeding us."

"Holy horse hockey!" Ereth snapped. "I know you're hungry. But if you go ambling around you're liable to get killed."

"I don't believe you," Tumble said. "You just like to boss us about. Mum didn't boss us. Dad doesn't."

"Look here, you leaky lump of wallaby filigree, if you want to get yourself snaffled by a trap, that's your business!"

"You old . . ." Tumble started to say, but shut his mouth when Ereth glared at him.

"Don't pay attention to him," Nimble said to the porcupine. "He's always grumpy."

"What . . . what can we do about the traps?" Flip asked.

Ereth turned to stare out over the field. It looked so free of all danger. Yet he knew that lurking beneath the snow was something truly deadly.

Turning back to the three cubs he said, "We have to find those traps."

"My dad could find them, easy," Tumble said.

"Fine, anthill brain," Ereth snapped. "Go and find your father. He can deal with it. That'll suit me perfectly. I'll be gone so fast you won't even remember I was here."

Tumble, backing off, muttered, "He's probably very busy . . ."

"We could throw some more rocks," Nimble suggested.

"That might work," Ereth agreed, "but only if we're lucky. If we're even just a bit off, it won't do us any good." He gazed at the huge expanse of snow again as if it could offer some answers.

"What . . . what about a snowball?" Flip asked timidly.

"That's stupid," Tumble said immediately.

But Nimble asked, "What do you mean?"

"Well . . . I was just thinking," Flip went on cautiously, looking from his brother to his sister and ignoring Ereth, "we could roll a ball in front of us, and, you know, keep it rolling. If it hit a trap it wouldn't hurt us — just the snowball. And . . . and I think it would leave a path we could walk on."

The foxes turned to Ereth.

The porcupine considered for a moment. Then he nodded vigorously. "Slug salad! That's a great idea. Best I've heard in a long time."

Flip grinned with pleasure.

"I think it's dumb," Tumble said.

Ereth paid him no mind. "Come on," he urged. "Roll up a ball right now and push it down the bluff."

Flip, delighted to have his idea so quickly put into practice, used his paws to shape a ball. Nimble helped. Very soon they had a large, if lopsided, ball of snow.

"That'll never roll," Tumble announced.

"Give it a try," Ereth urged.

Standing by the entryway to the den, Flip prodded the ball with his nose, managing to nudge it enough so that it began to roll down the bluff. As it went it gathered snow and speed. In its wake it left a wide path which exposed the earth. Very quickly it reached the bottom of the bluff.

"See?" Tumble said smugly. "No traps."

"That's the whole point, hippo head!" Ereth snapped. "At least we can walk down that way." This they did in single file, using the path the snowball had made, with the porcupine leading the way. When they came to the bottom, where the ball rested, they stopped. Having gathered snow during its roll, the ball was very much bigger.

"Now," Ereth commanded, "push the ball back toward the other den. Where I first met you."

Flip stood up on his hind legs and placed his front paws near the top of the ball. Nimble did the same.

As usual, Tumble held back. "There's no room for me," he announced.

"Just push," Ereth said to Flip and Nimble, as he added his own weight to the effort.

The three proceeded to roll the ball forward. The heavier ball was much harder to push. Even so it inched along. Suddenly, there was a loud *snap!* The ball exploded. The stunned foxes – as well as Ereth – jumped back.

Ereth, his face white with snow, peered cautiously forward. There, amid the remains of the snowball, was another trap, its teeth clenched ferociously together.

"Thirteen to go," the porcupine announced. There was relief in his voice, but also worry.

Tumble edged forward, sniffed the trap, then

touched it gingerly with a paw. He said nothing.

"What do we do now?" Flip asked.

Ereth sighed. "Make another snowball," he said.

At that Tumble barged forward and rolled up a new ball. Then he began to push it forward with his nose. "Come on," he called hotly to his brother and sister. "I need some help. Don't be so lazy."

The others joined in. Slowly they moved the ball along the base of the bluff. As it went forward it gathered more snow. It was after they had gone some thirty more feet that another trap sprung.

"Twelve," Ereth said. He looked around anxiously. "Is the area along the base of this bluff where you and your mother walked a lot?" he wanted to know.

"I suppose so," Nimble said.

"Well that explains one thing," Ereth said.

"What's that?"

"It wasn't an accident they caught your mother. Those trappers — those humans — were *trying* to snare you foxes."

"But . . . why would they do that?" Flip asked, his voice full of astonishment.

"Your fur," Ereth said glumly.

The foxes inspected their coats in puzzlement.

"Okay," Ereth said. "Let's put together another ball, and this time we'll roll it up the bluff to the entry of your regular den."

"Up there?" Tumble cried. "Up the bluff? That's too hard!"

"Go lick a lemon tree," Ereth snapped. "We don't have any choice."

It took all four of them to push the snowball up the face of the bluff. It was extremely hard work. More than once they ran into boulders and had to manipulate the increasingly heavy ball around them. Once it got away from them and rolled back to the bottom of the bluff, forcing them to start again.

At last, however, they reached the main den, without uncovering any more traps.

"Well," Ereth said. "At least you can go from one den to the other without any danger."

"But . . . Ereth . . ." Nimble asked plaintively, "what about food?"

Ereth sighed and looked back over the field again. He too was very hungry. He would have given anything to get back into the forest where the bark was plentiful. Instead he said, "We'll have to mark out more paths first. A lot of them. Otherwise it won't be safe."

Neither Flip nor Nimble objected.

But Tumble said, "You're all too slow. I know what to do." Before anyone could object, he scrambled down to the base of the bluff along the path that had just been cleared. Ereth and the other two foxes watched him go.

"Why is he always so crabby?" Ereth demanded.

Nimble exchanged looks with Flip.

"He misses Dad a lot," Flip blurted out. "I mean, we do too. But that's all Tumble ever talks about. You know, how he wishes Dad would come home."

A glum Ereth made no response. He merely watched Tumble.

At the base of the bluff the young fox was hastily putting together another ball of snow. Then, using his nose as well as his front paws, he began to shove it erratically across the field in the direction of Dimwood Forest. Clearly frustrated, he did not always stay behind the ball.

Ereth watched in dismay. "That worm wit is going to get himself killed," he said. With that he turned to the other two foxes. "Stay here," he commanded. Slipping and sliding, he scurried down the bluff after Tumble.

"Hey, wait!" he called.

Tumble did not even look around, but continued to roll his snowball forward.

Ereth, breathless from the exertion, caught up with the young fox. "Hey, you putrefying packet of parsnip pips, didn't you hear me?"

Tumble paid no attention. Instead, with his back to the porcupine, he struggled even harder with the ever-growing ball of snow, stubbornly inching it forward.

"Don't you understand?" Ereth cried after him. "This is dangerous work. Listen to me. You're going to get yourself killed."

Suddenly Tumble let go of the snowball, turned, and snapped, "Why don't you leave me alone! You're such a know-it-all. I'm sick and tired of being ordered around by you. Who are you? Nobody. We never asked you to come around here in the first place. We were perfectly fine until you stuck your nose in. Why don't you just go away? That'll make everybody happy."

"Do you think I *want* to be here?" Ereth roared

back. "Let me tell you something, cheese blister. I've got three billion better things to do. I'm only here because your mother asked me."

"She did not!"

"Suffocating snake slime! Why else would I have come here? She said you were helpless. That you needed me to look after you. That you couldn't get by on your own."

"That's not true!" Tumble shrilled, eyes hot with tears. Furious, he spun about and resumed pushing the snowball across the field, away from Ereth.

Ereth followed right after him.

When Tumble, with a darting glance over his shoulder, saw Ereth was at his heels, he cried, "We're old enough to be on our own. The only reason you came to us was to get out of the snow, get warm, and eat our food. You're just too lazy to go back to your own home. You're nothing but an old, ugly, fat porcupine. And you stink, too!"

Ereth, taken aback by the new onslaught of words, stopped in his tracks. For a moment he was speechless.

"See?" Tumble went on. "You insult whoever you want, but you can't take it, can you?

"Didn't you hear me? We don't need you," Tumble insisted, going forward again. "My sister and brother feel the same way, only they're too nice to say it. Well, I'm *not* nice or polite. I say what I think. Anyway, my father will get here soon and when he does, you can — "

At that precise moment the snowball exploded, hurling snow into Tumble's face.

The young fox, taken by surprise, stood in place, trembling. Poking up through the snow were the sharp steel jaws of another trap.

"There," Ereth said angrily. "Didn't I tell you to be careful?"

Tumble whirled around. "Oh, can't you ever be quiet!" he said into Ereth's face. Then he burst into tears.

Ereth blinked. "But what . . . what's the matter?"

The fox couldn't speak. He was sobbing too hard.

"Talk!" Ereth barked.

"I . . . want my mum . . ." Tumble whispered. "So badly. I miss her so much . . . "

Ereth paled. "But . . . she's . . ."

"I know she's dead!" Tumble cried, switching back to anger, though the tears continued to flow. "Stop telling me things I know. Oh, why don't you just go away! You're horrid to have around. You're bossy. You're sarcastic. And do you know what you are most of all? You're so old your brain has turned grey. Yeah, that's what you are. Old!" With that Tumble lifted his nose, opened his mouth wide and began to howl. "I want my daddy!" he cried again and again.

An appalled Ereth looked back over his shoulder to see if Flip and Nimble were watching and listening. To his great relief they were nowhere in sight. He could only hope they had gone down into the safety of the den and had not witnessed any of this.

Ereth turned back to Tumble. The young fox was just sitting there, his head low, looking miserable.

"Tumble . . ." Ereth began, not knowing what else to say.

"Go away!" the fox screamed, not looking up. "I hate you. I wish you were dead!"

"I'm just . . ." Ereth looked around again to see if anyone else was listening. When he saw no one he said, "I'm just trying to help."

"We don't need your help!" Tumble bayed.

Ereth sighed. "Someone had to tell you about your mother."

"Right. But you just barged in and blurted it out like the stupid animal you are. I mean, it was our mother, not yours!"

Cringing, Ereth struggled to find a reply. "But," he finally got out, "you needed to know about the traps, didn't you?"

"I . . . suppose," Tumble conceded through renewed sobs. "But now that Flip — not you — worked out a way to find them, you're not necessary."

"What . . . what about food?" Ereth asked.

"We don't like vegetables!" Tumble cried. "We like meat! But you don't hunt. So you're as useless as . . . as parboiled pumpkin puke!"

Shocked, Ereth's mouth opened wide but no words came out. The next moment he sputtered, "That's it. I give up. Do what you want. Drop dead for all I care!" With that, he pushed past Tumble and began to stumble through the snow toward Dimwood Forest.

Tumble did not look around, but continued to stare down at his feet and the exposed trap just a few inches away. Only when he was certain that Ereth had gone by did he lift his head and gaze after the retreating porcupine.

"Goodbye," Tumble whispered. The tears began to flow again.

"Salamander-sap salad!" Ereth cried as he breasted through the snow in the direction of the forest. Deeply upset, he was breathing heavily, snorting wrath with every trembling step he took. "Try and help idiots and it gets idiotic," he reminded himself. "Kill yourself for kids, and they'll kill you first. Ungrateful, spoiled brats! Rubbish to all children with a squashed boll weevil on top. Let 'em do what they want. They aren't *my* responsibility."

He paused and looked around to see where he was going. "I'll go back into the forest the way I came, get myself some decent food, then head right for that log cabin. Gobble up some salt. I mean, why should I care about a bunch of bungling, unappreciative babies . . ." Ereth, swearing all the while, pushed steadily across the field.

From his lookout on the aspen tree branch, Marty the pine marten spied Ereth moving toward the forest. "At last!" he cried, barely able to suppress his excitement. "I knew I was right to wait. And he's coming in my direction. Well, Ereth, you're in for one big Marty the pine marten surprise."

With that, the pine marten checked to make sure he was certain of the exact spot where Ereth would enter the forest. Then he scrambled down from his tree and raced for a hiding place. "Now I've got him!" he exulted.

18

Ereth Has Some Other Thoughts

Ereth was halfway across the field on his way to the forest when he suddenly came to a stop. "Bouncing balls of beeswax!" he muttered with horror. "The traps! I'm so furious I've forgotten all about them. I'm acting blind and brainless. Any moment now I could be stepping right into one of those things. If I do I'll maim myself. Kill myself!"

Anxiously, he swung about and took a step back along the trail he'd made through the snow. He had been, he now realised, lucky to come as far as he had without harm. It would be best to return. By walking in the same steps he had just made, he could get safely back.

But no sooner did he take one step back than he spied Tumble. The young fox, head low, was walking slowly toward the den. Just to see him filled Ereth with rage.

"Monkey marbles!" he shouted out loud. "No way I'm going back there." With that he spun about and faced the trees, only to have his nerves fail him again. "But if I'm caught in a trap . . .

"I know: I'll make a snowball, just the way those idiot cubs did. If I have to, I'll push it all the way home."

Ereth set about to shape a ball, only to quickly realise his legs were too short for the job.

"Great galloping guppy gunk!" he cried with a rage that brought tears to his eyes. "I don't know which way to go!" Trembling, Ereth stood in the middle of the field facing the forest. More than anything else, he wanted to lose himself in the trees, then find a way back to his own lovely log. How he yearned to return to his gloomy, stinky home, to wallow in his own muck, to have a soothing talk with Poppy. Oh, to be anywhere but where he was!

And yet, he could not make himself go forward. He was too afraid. Better to go back to the safety of the den. No! He didn't want to do that either. The cubs hated him. Didn't want him. He turned about. Even as he stood there, a breeze swept across the field, carrying snow. To his horror, the tracks he had just made began to disappear. If he didn't go back immediately he'd have to break a new trail, with the danger of stepping into a trap.

One moment Ereth was in a rage. The next moment he felt soft and weepy. What was happening to him? His helplessness was frightening. "Oh, sloth-swill soup with bird-drop stuffing!" he shouted to the air. "I can't go anywhere!"

Then all of a sudden an even more terrible thought came to him. What . . . what if . . . even *some* of the things Tumble had said were true? Could he really be so dreadful? Was he really a bad creature? Had he, in fact, become old without noticing?

The answer came in the form of a cold shiver that went through his whole body. Yes, it *was* so. Everything the young fox had said was true. He *was* an awful creature. He *was* old. He *was* bossy. No one bothered about his birthday because he wasn't worth bothering about. What's more, there was nothing he could do about it. He was too set in his ways to change. He was worthless. He might as well be dead. Ereth shut his eyes against his thoughts.

"Ereth . . . ?"

At first Ereth was not sure he heard his name. But the call came again, slightly more insistent.

"Ereth?"

Someone was calling to him.

Ereth opened his eyes. No one in front of him. Nor to either side. He looked back. It was Flip.

In spite of himself, Ereth scowled.

Flip stood some way off, afraid to come any closer.

"Ereth . . . ?" he called again cautiously. It sounded like a question, as if he were unsure he should even say the name.

Ereth felt his anger returning. "What is it?" he growled.

"Can . . . can I talk to you . . . ?"

"About what, tinkle brain?" the porcupine said, though he immediately regretted having spoken so.

"Ereth . . . Tumble came back to the den."

"What about it?"

"He . . . he told us what he said to you. He's very upset."

Ereth thought of saying, "What about *me?*" but held his tongue.

"He said that he yelled at you," Flip went on. "That he said a lot of . . . awful things. That he made you go away."

Ereth grunted.

"I . . . I just wanted to tell you that what he said isn't . . . the way Nimble and I . . . feel."

Ereth, unprepared for the searing pain he felt, stared at the young fox. Turning, he shifted away from Flip and gazed longingly at the forest.

Flip drew a little closer. "Ereth," he called. "I'm . . . I'm glad you came to us. I like you."

Ereth sniffed.

"I . . . wish you'd come back . . . " Flip coaxed. "We found three more traps."

"You did?" Ereth said.

"How many did you say there were?" Flip asked.

After a moment Ereth said, "Tumble just found another one. With the one you found before it adds up to six altogether. Then there was the one your Mum . . . found. Those trappers said they had put down sixteen. If we can believe them, that means there's just nine left."

"We could find them," Flip said. "I'm sure we could. But, Ereth, don't you think it would be better if you stayed with us?"

Ereth continued to face the forest. Perhaps he should live alone, the way he had spent most of his life before he met Poppy. When he was alone no one hurt him. No one ignored him. Being alone was safe.

"I mean, maybe you could just stay until our dad gets back," Flip said.

"Caterwauling catfish," Ereth cried. "For all you know he may never come back."

"Oh, sure he will," Flip said. "He cares for us a lot. He does. It's just that he's very busy. I mean, he has to take care of his business."

"What about *my* business?"

"Ereth," Flip pleaded. "Tumble is very upset. I don't think he meant what he said."

Ereth sighed.

"Did you hear me?" Flip asked.

"Maybe . . . it was true," Ereth whispered.

"Well, even if what he said was . . . a *little* bit true . . . Please, I still think we need you."

Ereth turned around and faced him. "You really want me to stay?"

"Yes."

Ereth sighed. "All right. But only until we find the rest of the traps. Or till your father gets back. Whichever comes first."

"Oh, wow. That's so great of you," Flip said excitedly. "I'll go tell the others." With that he turned and bounded back along the trail toward the den. He had not gone ten steps when he stopped and returned to Ereth.

"Now what?" Ereth demanded.

"There's something else I want you to know."

"What?" Ereth said, preparing for the worst.

"I really like you," Flip said. "I mean, you're really . . . sweet." With that the young fox hurried on back to the den.

Ereth stared after the young fox. Reaching up, he touched his nose on the spot where Poppy had once kissed it. "Sweet," he muttered with a grimace. "*Sweet* is a word for nitwits and gumdrops. . . . Not . . . me.

"It'll only be for a short time," he told himself. "A very short time." With that he began to waddle back along the trail Flip had just made, telling himself that it was, after all, the safest way to get anywhere.

Marty the pine marten watched with bitter disappointment as Ereth headed back toward the bluff.

"He's gone back to them," he growled. "That means I'm going to have to find some other way to get him alone."

He thought for a while. Then he smiled.

"Maybe it's time I found father fox. Yes, I think I'll let Bounder know exactly what's going on. He'll flush that stupid porcupine out."

With that thought, Marty whirled about and raced into the forest.

19
In Search of Food

When Ereth reached the den, the three foxes were sitting side by side near the entry-way. Suddenly uncomfortable, Ereth gazed at them. Nimble and Flip returned his look. Tumble avoided eye contact altogether.

For a moment no one said anything.

It was Nimble who called, "Hi, Ereth, where've you been?"

"Out," Ereth said. "Walking."

"Oh."

"See anything interesting?"

"No."

Silence.

"Listen here," Ereth snapped, "you tasteless tubs of toad twaddle, if you think . . ." Hearing himself, Ereth paused, cleared his throat, and began again. "What I mean is that if you willow wallows think I'm going to do all the work, while you loaf and soak up the sun like a bunch of cross-eyed octopuses — No! I didn't mean that. I . . ."

"What would you like us to do?" Flip said. "Chores? Hunt? Clean up? Whatever you say, Ereth. We'll be glad to do it."

"How about making some more snowballs?" Ereth continued testily. "Start rolling them along the base of the bluff, then go across the field in any direction you want. Just stay *behind* the balls. Do you understand? *Behind!*

"If there are any trails you and your mother used a lot, make sure you roll the balls those ways. Any questions? Problems? None? Good. Then get going!"

Yapping and braying, the foxes hurried down along the trails they had already made, packed up some new snowballs, and began to roll them in different directions.

When the three foxes returned to the den and Ereth, they were exhausted but elated.

"We found three more traps," Nimble cried with glee as she bounded up the bluff.

"Fine," Ereth said. "Good. We're making progress. It won't be long before you've found them all. We just need to search some more."

"Ereth . . ." It was Tumble who spoke.

"What?"

"We're really starving."

"Mum always brought home lots," Nimble added plaintively.

"More than we could eat," Flip agreed.

"More?" Ereth's ears perked up.

"There were times," Tumble said, "she brought us rabbits so big we couldn't even finish everything."

"What happened to the extra?" Ereth asked. "Did she take them off and eat the rest herself?" He knew that's what he would have done.

Flip shook his head. "Mum said dinnertime was family time, that it was rude to go off and eat alone. So we always ate together."

"Then, where did she put the leftovers?"

The foxes looked at one another in puzzlement.

"We don't know," Nimble said with a shrug. "She just did what she did."

"Do you think she could have stored them somewhere?" Ereth asked. "She ever mention having still another den? You know, an emergency storehouse?"

"She never said," Flip replied.

A frustrated Ereth turned to look over the

field. If there was a storage den stuffed with food it would make all the difference in the world. The problem was, such a place was likely to be well hidden. It could be *anywhere*.

He turned back to the waiting cubs. "There must be one. I think we'd better go and look for it," he said. "The point is, I can't teach you anything about hunting. But you need food. So think hard. Did your mother even hint about another place?"

"Nope," Nimble said.

"Okay," Ereth said. "Then here's what we're going to do. We've got those trails you've made. Instead of looking for traps, go back along them. Keep your noses to the ground. Sniff. Smell. See if you can find a storehouse. But, whatever you do, *don't go off the safe trails!* If you think you smell something, come back and we'll investigate together."

The cubs needed no further encouragement. They bounded off, each one going in a different direction.

As he waited, Ereth scrutinized the field, trying to guess where, if *he* were to build a secret storehouse, he might put it.

Then he craned around to look behind him, at

the crest of the bluff in particular, which rose up some five feet over his head. He doubted if the cubs would even think of looking there. A shrewd mother like Leaper, knowing that, might well put a storehouse in just such an out-of-the-way spot.

Ereth eyed the area carefully, trying to work out a way he could haul himself to the top. It was steep. But as he looked around he noted that not very far from where he sat was a natural cleft worn into the face of the bluff. If he could work his way up that cleft, he should be able to get beyond the bluff.

Still he hesitated. What about traps? There were still six to be uncovered. So far, however, they had all been found along the base of the bluff, in the forest, or out in the field. That suggested they wouldn't be beyond the bluff. Maybe.

Ereth looked over the field. The cubs remained hard at work. Should he tell them what he was doing? No. It would take too long. Besides, it would be a lot more enjoyable to greet them with news of his discovery – if he made one.

Ereth headed for the cleft, working his way across the bluff. It was not easy to reach. First there was snow with which to contend. Then too, the face of the bluff was studded with rocks and boulders, all of which slowed him down. More than once Ereth needed to stop and rest.

Once he reached the lower end of the cleft, he started up, clawing and scratching at the loose gravel and snow. Twice he had to stop, panting heavily. But when he pulled himself over the final bit, he faced a stand of pine trees. His heart skipped a beat. Food! Trailing drools of spit and ignoring all caution, he ran right towards the trees.

Upon reaching the pines he attacked them with nothing less than savagery, ripping away the outer layers of bark to get at and gnaw at the sweet under-bark.

After twenty minutes of nonstop eating, Ereth felt so stuffed, so crammed full of food, he had to rest and allow himself to digest his meal. Then, with a start, he recalled his original mission: food for the cubs.

He sat up and looked about. The first thing he realised was that there were enough trees in the area to keep him satisfied for a long time. That is to say, *his* food problem had been solved.

But where, he asked himself again, if he were a fox, would he place a secret den?

Ereth searched among the trees. The ground was hard, frozen in spots, though without many rocks. The snow was sparse here, and he was able to make his way with relative ease. Still, there didn't seem to be any logical place for a secret den.

Then he noticed, within a tightly woven grove of trees, a large pile of rocks. He lumbered over to it and eyed it with care, searching for a hole or anything to suggest an entry to an inner cache of food. But though he walked completely around the pile, he saw nothing that even hinted at it.

He was about to move on when he decided he should climb atop the pile. Perhaps – though he doubted it – he might see something more from up there.

He clambered up the rocks. It was not easy, and he kept swearing to himself. Then, as he climbed higher, he began to detect the smell of something distinctly unpleasant.

Ereth reached the top of the pile, and suddenly the smell of meat was much more pungent. Poking about the top, he found a hole. It was not a very large hole, but when he put his nose to it he had to jump back, so repellent was the stench. It was the stink of meat. A *lot* of meat.

Excited now, Ereth scratched about the hole, trying to enlarge it. The edges gave way quickly, as if they had been but loosely packed in the first place.

Very soon Ereth was able to poke his head down into a bigger hole. What Ereth saw in the dim light made him blink. The pile of rocks enclosed an entire storeroom of food: partially eaten rabbits, voles, chipmunks, and even, to his horror, mice. All were frozen.

It was as he had guessed and hoped: Leaper *had* carefully provided emergency rations for her family to last for a good part of the winter. No one would starve.

Caught between total revulsion and complete glee, Ereth wheeled about and dashed back towards the bluff and the foxes. "Bouncing bear burps!" he cried, "I've found it. We're saved." He was so excited he hardly noticed he was using the word "we."

20

Bounder

Towards the other end of Dimwood Forest was a small, shallow glen. All but circular in shape, the hollow was surrounded by tall pines, their heavy limbs bent with snow. Near the centre of the place – like the hub of a wheel – was a rock. Atop the rock, bathing in the warm sun beneath the blue sky, was a large, handsome fox. It was Bounder, the father of the three cubs.

Head high, majestic tail curled about his body, Bounder was in perfect repose. His coat of ruby red fur was as thick as summer grass. His paws were powerful. His noble face, long and pointed, bore deepset eyes and sharp whiskers.

Indeed, he was quite prepared to believe that the rock upon which he rested and even the sun in the sky were there for him, so as to show him at best advantage. All that was missing was a pool of water in which he might admire his own image.

A few days ago Bounder had heard a rumour

that the humans at New Farm – at the eastern end of Dimwood Forest – had built a brand-new chicken coop. The coop was full of plump chickens – or so the fox had been informed. With visions of many tasty meals in his future, the fox was determined to visit the coop. Just thinking about it made him lick his lips in anticipation. For Bounder did what he wanted, how he wanted, when he wanted. It was only the snowstorm that had interrupted his journey.

Though the storm was now over and he was still planning to go, the soothing sun upon his back detained him. The warmth provided such sweet contentment, he had shut his eyes and given himself over to random thoughts.

Even as the fox's eyes were shut, his ears were working, listening to the sounds of the forest, on guard for the slightest hint of any disturbance to which he should attend.

As time went by he caught the sound of a mouse burrowing under the snow. Bounder decided the mouse was not big enough for him to bother with.

Not long after that, he was certain a baby rabbit was hopping by the rock. Though the fox knew the rabbit was easy prey, once again he decided that the animal's small size did not justify making any effort to catch it.

It was his awareness of the young rabbit, however, that caused him to think — momentarily — about his wife, Leaper, and his three cubs, Nimble, Tumble, and Flip.

Regarding Leaper, Bounder had no great depth of feeling. When he thought of her, it was to acknowledge that she was a good mother to these cubs of his. That, as far as he was concerned, was the only thing important about her. For Leaper's good mothering meant that he, Bounder, did not have to concern himself very much about his youngsters. That in turn allowed him to go about his business freely without the least hindrance. And so he did.

As for the cubs, he did care for them, but on his own terms. He enjoyed visiting them from time to time. He liked to bring them special treats, like a freshly killed chicken — something their mother would not risk providing. He also enjoyed engaging the cubs in a bit of rough play — just enough to let them experience *his* strength.

But what Bounder liked most, in regard to his cubs, was to allow his children to gaze upon him with adoring eyes. Once that was accomplished, he would go off again on his private business.

All that, in Bounder's opinion, was the proper life for a father fox.

So it was that as the fox continued to lie beneath the warm sun, he deliberately dismissed thoughts of home and family. Life was too good for him to be disturbed by such things.

But then Bounder heard the sound of something much larger than a baby rabbit. Opening his orange eyes a little, he sought out who it might be. There, on a branch on one of the trees overlooking the glen, was Marty the pine marten.

As soon as the fox realised it was Marty, he shut his eyes again. Bounder did not like Marty. As far as the fox was concerned, the pine marten was an unpleasant creature: sly, secretive, not always to be trusted.

"Hello, Bounder," Marty called out. "Do you know what is happening?"

The fox said nothing.

"Well, then," the pine marten said, "my guess is that you don't want to know what's happened to your wife, Leaper, and those three cubs of yours who go by the names Tumble, Nimble, and Flip."

Bounder felt uneasy. By stating the fox's family's names, Marty had aroused his curiosity. Still, the last thing the fox wanted to do was *ask* for the story. That would put someone else in control, a thing Bounder did not like to happen. He preferred to be in charge.

When the fox neither moved or replied, Marty called, "It's a pretty tragic tale, Bounder. I don't blame you for not wanting to know."

Bounder continued to act with indifference.

"But then," Marty continued loudly, "since everyone else knows what happened, I suppose you do too. Yes, I'd guess you were the first one to hear. Well, Bounder, you *do* have my sympathy."

Bounder, no longer able to resist, turned to the pine marten. "I beg your pardon. Were you talking to me?" He was very vexed, but worked hard to avoid showing it.

"Of course I was talking to you," Marty cried. "And you heard everything I said, didn't you? You foxes have a great reputation for listening. I suppose you're as good as most. Better, maybe."

Bounder sniffed loudly a few times. "Listening?"

he said. "Actually, my hearing hasn't been very good lately. A kind of cold or . . . something. The snowstorm, I suspect. Even so, if you have something to say to me, I'd be happy to make an effort to hear it."

Marty studied Bounder intently with his dark, emotionless eyes, trying to make up his mind if the fox was telling the truth or not. He decided he was not. And that annoyed him. "It's your wife, Leaper," he called bluntly. "She's been killed."

"*Killed!*" Bounder cried, taken aback, but under such self-control that he remained in place. "You're lying!"

"No. It's true. By a hunter's steel trap. Near the cabin at Long Lake. It happened just yesterday, during the snowstorm."

"What about my cubs? Were they hurt?"

"Oh, no. They weren't with her."

"Do they know about her?"

"I'm not sure."

Now Bounder was concerned. "Tell me everything you know."

"All I know is that an old porcupine who goes by the name Ereth is staying with your cubs!"

"*Ereth!*"

"That's him. He seems to have moved into your den."

"In *my* den!" Bounder cried. "With *my* cubs?"

"I think so."

Bounder knew all about Ereth. If anything, he knew him too well. Little more than a year ago he had been chasing a mouse through the forest when she ran into a hollow log to escape. The log proved to be Ereth's home. Though all Bounder had wanted to do was to eat the mouse – porcupines, he knew, were not meat eaters – Ereth had slapped him with his tail, giving him a nose full of painful quills. So, yes, Bounder knew all about Ereth. He disliked him intensely.

"Those are *my* cubs," the fox growled. "That porcupine has no business with them, none. What's he doing there?"

"I think . . . " Marty the pine marten said, "he's pretending to be their . . . father."

"Their father!" Bounder exclaimed. "Are you making any of this up?"

"Not in the least. And quite a happy family they've become. That's all I know." So saying, Marty the pine marten retreated among the branches of the tree. He was deep enough for Bounder to lose sight of him, but not so far away that he could not watch the fox.

Bounder was thinking hard about what he had heard. "Could it really be true?" he asked himself. If true, it was a dreadful thing that had happened to Leaper. He truly regretted it. He did. But at least his cubs were safe and being cared for. As far as Bounder was concerned, that was the most important thing. Regarding Ereth the porcupine – Bounder grinned. It served the old porcupine right for being such a busybody. What a perfect revenge on Ereth – the old porcupine taking care of *his* cubs. Acting like their father. Until of course, he dismissed him.

The more Bounder thought about it, the more it pleased him that his old foe should be stuck with the job of taking care of his children. Served the porcupine right. Moreover, it meant that he, Bounder, could get on with his business of catching the chickens from the coop at New Farm.

With that thought Bounder trotted off through the snow, his mind entirely on those plump chickens.

"Good," Marty the pine marten said to himself as he watched Bounder go off. "If I know Bounder he'll get Ereth away from those cubs. And when the porcupine is alone again I'll be there, waiting for him."

21

Discoveries

It was now a whole week since Ereth had first come to the foxes' den. With a plenitude of food available, life had settled into a steady routine.

Sleeping arrangements were something of a compromise. While the cubs slept on their own heap of leaves, it worked out that Ereth slept there too. Sixteen paws, four tails, and countless quills found a way to be close without anyone's being hurt. What's more, everyone's sleep was sound.

Ereth was the first to get up each morning. Even as the sun threw golden shafts of light over the white field in front of the bluff, he could be found scrambling toward the grove of trees. There he breakfasted on tender bark, eating as much as he wanted. Only when he was fully satisfied did he return to the den to wake the cubs.

It was not an easy task. "Time to wake up, you slimy slugs!" he'd cry out, or something equally cheerful and inviting.

Nimble was usually the first to stagger up. A very sleepy Flip followed. As for Tumble, he almost had to be dragged to his feet. Even then he protested in his grumpy fashion all the way.

Once the three cubs were up, there was considerable yawning, stretching, and bumping, not to mention bickering. Ereth, meanwhile, snapped, ordered, cajoled, and otherwise insisted that faces be washed, fur groomed, tails smoothed. Nimble had the most trouble with this, insisting she did not care what anyone thought about how she looked, that she was going to appear as she chose no matter what. Flip went the other way. He took great pains with his grooming, insisting that there was no way he would be caught dead (his unfortunate words) looking anything less than exactly as he wished. As for Tumble, he did not care one way or the other, but simply went through the motions to avoid Ereth's barbs.

Though it seemed to take forever, everyone was eventually up and ready. Then one of the foxes was sent out to the storage den to fetch breakfast. Being chosen and sent by Ereth was considered something of a privilege. Ereth tried to be careful as to his choice, rewarding now one, now another for good behaviour, so no one was favoured unfairly.

Whoever went brought back just enough breakfast for the other two. Ereth's orders were always the same: "Take *only* as much as we really need," he insisted. "It has to last the rest of the winter."

While the morning's breakfast was devoured – with much smacking of lips, wagging of tails, and snapping of bones – Ereth made sure he went outside. Try as he might, he simply could not abide a meal with the foxes – neither the food they ate nor their manners – but had decided that they were not going to change. Protest was to no avail.

Once he sensed breakfast was done Ereth returned to the den. It was time for the daily chores. Everybody knew exactly what to do – not that it ever went smoothly or without complaint. If Flip was supposed to tidy the bed, it almost never failed that Tumble or Nimble messed his work up. If Nimble was smoothing down the den floor, there was Tumble or Flip to track it up. Tumble, whose job was the removal of odd bits of bone and uneaten food, almost inevitably discarded something that the other two were saving.

"You're nothing but a bunch of lazy-legged

leeches," Ereth would inform them hotly. "Why do you always have to be bothering and bickering with each other?"

The cubs, who had grown used to the way Ereth talked and groused, paid little attention to him, except to laugh. But once when Tumble, in imitation, actually called Ereth "a pillow of potted porcupine," Ereth was beside himself with indignation.

"You youngsters," he yelled, "are nothing more than a tribe of disrespectful renegades. All of you should be turned out in the dead of winter to fend for yourselves, and then, maybe, *maybe*, your brains would grow as fast as your appetites and that would make the world a better place."

The cubs just laughed.

Once the chores were done — and in the end they always did get done — they all went outside and began the daily search for the remaining unsprung traps.

The search began with a discussion as to what areas of the field they should investigate that day and how they should do it. There was even Dimwood Forest to consider.

Ereth, for one, was wary of the forest, fearful

of what might be found there. While he was fairly certain the hunters had not returned to the field, Ereth could not be certain about the forest. The problem was, if the hunters *had* returned, there was no way of knowing if new traps had been set. Though he kept it to himself, Ereth had a distinct memory of the traps he'd seen under the cabin, the four additional spring traps and the one designed to catch a large animal alive.

From time to time Ereth contemplated going back to the log cabin on his own. Once there, it would be easy to determine if the humans had returned. The idea was appealing. Besides, he had not forgotten the salt.

Yet it was the presence of the salt that held Ereth back. He preferred to keep that a secret. Not that he believed that the foxes had any interest in it. In fact he was certain they would never understand his feelings for salt at all.

Over the next six days they did find traps, four in all. By Ereth's reckoning, that meant — if the humans had spoken truly — there were only two more to find.

In the afternoons, Ereth insisted that the cubs

take naps. This they did while he took a brief stroll back out to the grove of trees, where once again he satisfied his own appetite.

After nap time, there was dinner to fetch.

The hours after dinner were the best. Snug and warm beneath the ground, feeling safe, their bellies full, the cubs settled down. Every night Ereth told the cubs stories. Mostly they were about things he had done or heard about. What they loved most were the exploits of Ereth's famous friend, Poppy. The cubs loved the tales about the many battles she and Ereth had fought. With eyes wide and large ears erect, they paid close attention to them all. Indeed, they liked these stories so much, no one objected when Ereth repeated them, even though each time the porcupine told them they grew in length, facts, complexity.

In turn, the foxes told stories about their mother and how she had hunted this or that creature. Though Ereth was not really interested, he listened patiently.

Not so pleasing for Ereth to hear were tales about Bounder, the foxes' father. These stories seemed all alike to him, tales in which Bounder accomplished the most amazing feats with incredible strength and astonishing brilliance.

"He's the smartest fox in the whole world," Nimble assured Ereth, when the porcupine dared to question whether Bounder had once truly managed to open a steel lock on a certain farmer's barn using only his teeth.

"How do you know it really happened?" Ereth asked.

"Because Dad told us, and what he says is true," Tumble said, defiance in his voice.

"Do you think he'd lie to us?" Flip demanded.

"Snail sauce on snake saliva," Ereth returned. "I was just asking."

At night, when the young foxes were finally in bed and Ereth was at peace, he sometimes thought about how different his life had become. How crowded. How busy.

From time to time, he also thought of his home and, in particular, of Poppy. It was a long while now since he had left his log. Ereth wondered if she ever puzzled as to what had happened to him. Did she miss him? Was she worried about him? Did she regret ignoring his birthday?

Just to think about such things made Ereth

unhappy. "Better to be here," he told himself. "At least the cubs are beginning to appreciate me."

Early one morning, when Ereth popped out of the den, he was startled to see two hunters walking about the field. Horrified, he watched as they moved along the trails the foxes had made. One by one they picked up the sprung traps and stowed them in a bag.

Ereth stayed to see if they would reveal the unsprung traps – or if they would put down new ones. They did neither, but retreated back into the woods.

The porcupine was not sure whether to be pleased by what he had observed. He could only hope they had not touched the salt at the cabin.

When he told the cubs about the hunters they listened wide-eyed. "The danger isn't over," he warned. "Not yet."

More cold winter days passed. There were good days and bad. Sometimes winter weather raged. Sometimes it was almost balmy. Even so, one more trap was discovered, leaving, by Ereth's calculations, just one more trap to be found. He was hopeful they would find that one soon enough.

One evening, four weeks from the time Ereth had first come to the cubs, right in the middle of what must have been his fourteenth telling of the famous battle between Mr Ocax the great horned owl and Poppy the mouse, a voice boomed down the entry tunnel.

"Anybody home?" the voice bayed. "Anybody care for some fresh chicken?"

There was a moment of silence.

Then Tumble leaped to his feet. "It's Dad!" he cried, and tore up the entryway. The next moment his sister and brother followed.

"Buzzard boozers on burnt toast," Ereth mumbled. "Bounder has returned." The old porcupine felt very nervous.

22

The Return of Bounder

Below ground Ereth could hear joyful yapping and barking from the cubs up above. Part of him wanted to go up and see what was happening. After hearing so many stories about Bounder from the cubs, he was curious about him and wondered what he was truly like. But he worried even more how the fox would treat him.

While Ereth hesitated, a very excited Flip rushed down into the den. "Ereth," he cried, "why are you staying down here? Come on up. It's Dad. He's back. Don't you want to meet him? And guess what? He brought a whole fresh chicken. Just for us. Isn't that fantastic? It's the best thing I've ever eaten! A lot better than anything Mum or you ever got us. Come on! Look!" With that, the excited fox raced back up to the surface.

Even as Ereth knew it was good that Bounder had returned, he wished the fox had not. Ereth was not unfamiliar with jealousy. He recognized the almost forgotten feeling in himself now. It infuriated him. "You pocket of pig poke," he accused himself. "You're an idiot! A fool! A dope!"

The force of his own barrage propelled him up the entry tunnel. Once at the top he poked his head out and looked around.

Bounder was stretched out on the ground, forepaws extended, tail straight behind him, head held high. There was an air of muscular pride about him as he gazed down at the cubs.

The three youngsters were frolicking before him, yapping and growling joyfully, tails wagging wildly. They were in the midst of devouring the chicken, which they must have pulled apart as soon as it was offered. But even as they ate, they kept breaking away from the food to leap at their father, pummel him with their paws, nip at his fur, roll on his back, then rush back to their food lest they miss a delicious morsel. All the while they also were — as best they could with mouths full — jabbering away, telling Bounder everything they had been doing. They talked simultaneously, paying no heed to one another. Ereth had never seen them so happy.

There was endless chatter about tracking down

the traps. "There were sixteen of them, Dad! Sixteen! They were so ugly. And really scary."

On they went: How Flip had the idea of making snowballs to find them safely. How they had managed to make the balls. How the balls had worked.

There was talk too about the big snowstorm and, in passing, the sad death of Leaper — but that talk was brief. There was much more talk about how they had managed to keep everything going. "Mum left us a whole storage den of food, Dad," Nimble explained. "So we've had plenty to eat."

"But this is so much better than anything she left!" Tumble quickly put in, his mouth full of chicken.

The only thing the cubs never mentioned was Ereth.

Bounder himself gave little response to the youngsters other than a few nods and yaps, just enough to make it apparent he was aware the cubs were talking to him.

Then, quite casually — as if by accident — Bounder turned and gazed at Ereth. Their eyes met. In an instant Ereth recognized him as the fox he had met in Dimwood Forest a long time ago, when Poppy had first run into his log.

He could not help but grin at the memory, telling himself he had every reason to detest this fox, and that nothing – ever – would alter that. Nothing.

"Well, hello, Ereth," Bounder said in a low, even voice. "What a surprise to see you here."

"Nice to see you again," Ereth returned, trying to keep the snarl out of his voice, but not quite managing.

Nimble, hearing the exchange, looked up and around. "Oh, right, Dad. This is Ereth. He's been staying with us."

"Has he?" Bounder said.

"Yeah," Tumble put in as he looked up from his food. "But don't worry. Now that you're back he'll go away. That's what he keeps telling us."

Ereth flinched.

It was Bounder who grinned now. "Been keeping warm in my den, Ereth?" he asked the porcupine.

"I've been taking care of your cubs," Ereth replied sharply. "Where have you been?"

"Oh, you know how it is, Ereth," the fox said in his most casual way. "Business. Constant business. It keeps me on the go. I wish I had the time to hang around and take it easy – like you," he added with a smile. "But then, some of us have to work hard to make a living."

"Dad," Tumble said. "Do you want to see how we make the snowballs and find the traps? Do you? Please. It was our own idea."

"Be delighted to, son," he said. "Delighted." He stood up to his full height. He was much bigger than the cubs, and Ereth too, for that matter.

The young foxes fell back and stared at him with wide-eyed admiration.

"Dad," Nimble said, her voice tinged with awe, "how big are you?"

"Oh, pretty big," the fox returned casually. "And someday you might be as big, too."

"As big as you?" Flip asked in astonishment.

"Could be. If you eat all the meat you can." He looked at Ereth. "We foxes are mostly meat eaters. You know, mice and such."

"Come on, Dad," Tumble cried. "I really want to show you how we get those traps."

"Be right there, son. You lot go ahead. I need to tell Ereth some things."

"Dad," Flip said.

"What?"

"I think you'd better stick to the paths we made. There's still one trap we haven't found. Isn't that right, Ereth?" He looked over to Ereth.

"Right," Ereth said glumly.

Flip, sensing something was wrong, cast a worried look at Ereth, then at his father before joining his brother and sister, who were already heading down the bluff.

Left alone, Ereth and Bounder eyed each other with suspicion and hostility. Ereth, to his own horror, found himself wishing he could be so big and handsome and young, instead of being so old, small, lumpish, and covered with quills.

"So you've been looking after my cubs," the fox said.

"Leaper asked me to."

Bounder lifted one eyebrow skeptically. "I thought she had passed away."

"I came upon her just before she died, broom tail," Ereth returned. "She was caught in a trap."

"Yes. Terribly sad."

"She asked me to come here, tell the cubs what happened, take care of them."

"Oh?" Bounder said, again conveying doubt.

Ereth felt rage boiling up inside him. "Yes, she did, actually, you lump of lizard lung," he shot back. "Only until you got back."

Bounder grinned. "Well, here I am."

"Are you going to stay with them?"

"Well, Ereth, I don't know if that's any of your business. They're my cubs. I think I can manage perfectly well without your intruding."

Ereth opened his mouth to say something. He found himself too furious, too upset to speak.

"Hey, Dad!" Tumble was calling from the base of the bluff. "Aren't you coming?"

"Be right there," Bounder called back. To Ereth, he said, "Look here, porky, I think it would be best if you left. Why don't you just take off right now. I'm going to be down there for a while. When we get back, I want you gone."

"But . . ."

"Hey, Ereth," Bounder said, "face it. It's me – their father – they should be with, not you. They don't care about you. Don't you see? You're no longer wanted. Or needed. In other words, pin cushion, you're fired." So saying, Bounder turned his back on Ereth, and with a whisk of the tail that managed to swipe across Ereth's nose, he trotted down the bluff.

Ereth, watching him go, felt as though he was suffocating with rage and humiliation. His eyes filled with tears. His chest was bursting with pain. "You dusty dump of dog diddle," he muttered furiously. "You stretched-out piece of wet worm gut! You bottomless barrel of leftover camel spit! You . . ." He was so enraged he could speak no more.

Even so, for a while Ereth remained where he was, staring down the hill, watching the cubs frolic with their father. Then, still boiling with a furious hurt, he retreated to the entryway, only to realise that was the last place he should be.

"I can't go without saying goodbye to the cubs," he told himself. "I can't. And there's nothing that idiot of a fox can do to prevent me from doing that."

With that Ereth made his way along the bluff until he reached the cleft in its side. From there he scurried over the bluff, after which he made his way to Leaper's winter food stockpile.

Once among the trees, the old porcupine chewed on some bark strips, but quickly realised he had lost his appetite. Instead of eating he climbed into a tree in search of sleep. In the morning he would talk to the cubs – if they came – alone.

23
Ereth Says Goodbye

It was the first time in a long time that Ereth had slept outside and he made a poor night of it. Tossing and turning, more than once he almost fell off his perch. He kept waking and craning about to look for the first signs of dawn. Again and again there were none.

Sometimes he felt full of rage. At other moments he was so full of grief he almost could not see. Ereth's thoughts kept turning to his old life of solitude, before the cubs, before Poppy, before these ridiculous feelings, all of which were a direct result of too much contact with other creatures.

"There are other places to live besides Dimwood Forest," Ereth told himself. "I'll find one and make sure no one ever sees me again. And I'll never leave that home. Never, never, never."

Dawn came at last. When it was little more than a pale pink glimmering along the eastern horizon, Ereth scrambled down from the tree. He went directly to the pile of rocks, trusting that one of the cubs would show up sooner or later to get some food.

Exactly what he intended to say if anyone appeared, he had no idea. All he knew was that he had to say *something*. He did caution himself not to say anything bad about Bounder. It would get him nowhere. Worse, it would only, in all probability, anger the cubs. Nothing would be gained.

As time passed Ereth tried to wait patiently, but found himself pacing. Around and around the pile he went, pausing now and again to check the progression of the sun in the sky. It was growing late. Humph! If he were at the den those cubs would have been up and about a long time ago.

Then he asked himself what he would do if they did *not* come. "No, they have to come," he kept telling himself. "But what if they don't?" he wondered. Should he stay the whole day and wait until the next? No! If they did not come soon he would do what he needed to do, which was to find a new home for himself.

When the cubs finally came — about an hour and a half later — Ereth was daydreaming about burrowing deep inside a dark, smelly log.

Startled by a sound, he swung about. Nimble, Tumble, and Flip were right before him, sitting in a row. They were looking at him. Their tails were wagging, their mouths slightly open, their large ears pricked forward.

"Ereth!" Flip said. "We didn't expect to see you here."

"Where did you think I'd be, murk mind?"

"Well, Dad said you wanted to get home right away," Nimble explained. "And that's why you didn't say goodbye."

"Is that what he said?"

"Yeah," Tumble said.

Ereth took a deep breath. There was a great deal he felt like saying. All he said, however, was, "That isn't true. He told me to go. How come you're all here?" he asked.

Tumble said, "Dad said we should have a huge breakfast together. Told us to come up and grab as much as we wanted. A feast. As much as we could carry. That's why."

Ereth said nothing.

"Ereth," Flip asked cautiously, *"are* you going home?"

"Eventually," Ereth returned. "But I needed to hang around."

"Why?" Nimble asked.

"I . . . I wanted to say goodbye."

"Oh," Flip said.

"Did you think I'd go without that?" Ereth demanded angrily.

The foxes exchanged looks, but said nothing. They had ceased wagging their tails.

As Ereth considered them, he thought they seemed a little sad. Or were they only confused? Or did he only want them to have those feelings? Maybe they were just embarrassed. Maybe they were wishing he had not been there. Flip kept looking over his shoulder, back toward the bluff, as if half expecting his father to appear.

"Look here," Ereth began, though he found it hard to speak. "I just wanted to say . . . I liked being . . . with you."

"It . . . was fun," Flip said after a moment.

"Fun . . ." Ereth echoed sadly before continuing. "I . . . really came to . . . well . . . like you. You taught me a . . . lot."

"Taught *you*?" Tumble asked. "What could we teach you?"

"Oh . . . forget it," Ereth muttered helplessly. "I

only wanted to say," Ereth repeated, "that I'm glad I stayed. You're very . . . nice."

"I'm glad you think so," Nimble said, giving a slight wag of her tail.

"And . . . and," Ereth struggled, "if you ever, well, need me for anything, you can come and get me."

"You never told us where you lived," Flip said.

"Cross the field, through the forest, till you get to the log cabin at Long Lake. Follow the trail south until you reach a grey snag. It's full of mice. I live right next to it. In a log."

"Great," Nimble said. "Maybe we'll visit you."

"Yeah, right," Ereth returned, not sounding very encouraging or hopeful. Then he remembered that he was going to find a new home where he could live alone, so no one would find him. He didn't let them know about that.

No one spoke. The foxes gazed at Ereth, then away, then down at their paws. Ereth, not trusting himself to look at them, stared at his paws too.

"I have to go," he suddenly announced. "Be careful until you find that last trap."

"Don't worry," Tumble said. "We will."

Still Ereth hesitated. "Hope things go well."

"We'll be okay," Nimble said.

"Okay," Ereth said. Abruptly he whirled about, took three steps and banged into a tree. "Puckered pine pits!" he screamed. Then he backed off and stumbled away.

After ten yards he stopped and turned around. The foxes were still sitting there. Still looking after him.

"One more thing," the porcupine croaked. "If I ever hear that any of you gangling idiots eats a mouse, I'm coming back. And if I do, I'll make your nose look like a cactus in need of a haircut! Remember that!"

With that, Ereth, not daring to look back, ran away as fast as he could.

24
Ereth and the Salt

Ereth waddled blindly through the woods. He barged into bushes, bumped into trees, slipped, stumbled, fell into pockets of snow. Each time he stalled, he snarled, swore under his breath, picked himself up, pawed his eyes clear, and pushed on.

Only when he grew so weary that he had to rest did he stop and lean against the trunk of a tree. He did so reluctantly, gasping for breath. Briefly, he peered back along the trail he had just travelled to see if he had been followed.

For a second, he thought someone *was* there, and his heart jumped. Then he decided he was just imagining things and his heart sank again.

With an angry shake of his head, he murmured, "Alone at last," and allowed himself a sigh that he fancied was one of contentment. At the same time he felt a great swell of emotion in his chest, which he did not have the energy to suppress. The effort left him weak and shaky.

"Blue heron hogwash," he muttered. "I'm done with all this family fungus! Better to do what I want, when I want, how I want. I'm free again! Life is *good!*"

With that Ereth gave himself a shake, as if he could rid himself of whatever might be sticking to his quills. "It's about time I did something for myself," he announced out loud. Then he grinned. "Time to get some . . . salt."

Damp-eyed, he looked around. By scrutinising the sun as well as the shadows on the ground, he determined where he was.

After careful consideration, Ereth was quite sure his headlong rush had taken him north. To the best of his judgment, Long Lake, along with the cabin and the salt, was to be found in a southwesterly direction.

Feeling much more composed, Ereth took time to eat before resuming his journey. Yet once, twice, he gazed about, unable to rid himself of the feeling that someone was lurking in the woods, watching him.

"Fool," he muttered. "No one's there! No one will ever be there!" Still, he allowed himself the thought that it was always best to be on guard. But when he caught himself taking another peek behind, he made a stern vow to look no more.

As he went on, his spirits grew lighter. It was good, he kept telling himself, to be on the move. Good to have no responsibilities other than himself. He tried to put his thoughts on the salt and how it would taste. He thought too about home — wherever that might be. Indeed, the old porcupine thought of many things, but never once did he allow himself to think of the cubs any longer than the moment it took to regret such thoughts. All that, he insisted to himself, was over and done with. Finished. Only once did he slip from his mental discipline, when he suddenly shouted, "They didn't even say thank you!" That said, he vowed to say no more. It was done. Gone. Finished. The end.

The porcupine pushed through the woods at a steady clip. The snow had receded, leaving great patches of brown, cold earth. The pine-scented air was bright and crisp, filled with buoyant energy.

When Ereth decided he had gone far enough to avoid the field and the bluff, he swung southwest, trusting that at some point he would reach the shores of Long Lake.

It was not till late afternoon that he rested again. Early winter shadows, like grasping paws, extended a stealthy hold over what remained of the crusty white snow.

The porcupine fueled himself with a quick chew of some bark, then set off again. "That lake should be near," he told himself, trying to ignore his exhaustion.

As he hurried, there were a few times — despite his earlier resolve — that he caught himself thinking about the cubs again. What had they done all day? Had they eaten well? Did they do their chores? Had they thought about him? Then, with a snarl and a muttered, "Salivating shrew slop," he angrily dismissed such thoughts and willed himself to concentrate on the salt that soon would be his.

He reached the lake at twilight. In the dim light its surface lay white and frozen. Ereth stared at it. It looked so cold and deserted.

Suddenly, tears began to flow. "Oh, why did I ever leave home?" he asked himself. "Because of my birthday," he recalled. "No one paid any attention to me. I was forced to go and get a present for myself. And look what's happened! Well, that'll be my last birthday. That'll teach 'em!" he said out loud with a savage bite in his voice.

"Salt," he whispered with desperation, "I must get some salt."

With new urgency, Ereth wheeled about and hurried on. Keeping the lake to his right, he skirted the shore. Sometimes, as he scooted across low, beach-like areas, the going was easy. At other times the shore was irregular or boggy, clotted with old brambles. In those places he had to push his way through or take long detours. "Why is it always so hard to get where you want to go?" he complained.

Night wore on. The white moon rose with brilliant promise, only to be obscured by clouds. A wind rattled the bare branches like old bones. Around midnight, snow began to fall. Fearful that if he stopped he might never move again, Ereth pressed on. The snow piled up quickly, making the going slower. When dawn came, grey and hard, mantled by still-falling snow, he dared not rest.

Then, at last Ereth saw the cabin. By early morning's thin light it seemed little more than a dark lump on the snow-filled landscape. No lights were on, though Ereth reminded himself that was no proof the hunters weren't there. It was still early. The humans might be sleeping.

He sniffed the air, trying to detect any hint of burning wood. None.

Emboldened, Ereth edged closer to the cabin. He continually looked about, seeking some sign, any sign, that would suggest the presence of people.

There were no footprints, but new snow would have covered them. Briefly, he tried to calculate the time since he'd seen the hunters on the field. Was it two weeks ago? A month?

In the growing daylight he scrambled under the cabin and peered around. No snowmobile. That, he decided, was a good sign.

Then he caught sight of the box in which he had seen the traps and was filled with revulsion. Even so, he crept forward, hoisted himself up, and peered inside. The box was empty.

Had the humans come back and set the remaining traps? Or had they returned and taken the traps away with them?

Cautiously, Ereth crept out from under the cabin and worked his way to the front porch.

He went up the steps and put his nose to the door jamb. A tremor of excitement coursed through him. The smell of salt was unmistakable. *It was still there!* His heart hammered. Oh, if only he could have some! So much would be mended!

He crawled up to the window, the one he had previously knocked in. Not only was glass back in place, bars had been placed over it. One glance and a disappointed Ereth knew there was no way he could get through it.

He dropped down and butted his head against the door. It would not give. Frantic, he raced down the steps and around the cabin, searching for any way to get inside. He found none. He even plunged under the cabin in hopes he might discover an entry there. Once again he was thwarted.

"Hit the puke switch and duck!" he shouted. "It's not fair. I deserve better. I've been treated badly. I should get *something!*"

Furious, feeling nothing but the cruel injustice of the world, he raced back to the front porch. Maybe he had given up on the window too quickly. In great haste, he crawled up and balanced himself on the windowsill. Perched precariously, he clutched the bars and tried to rattle them as if he were in a cage and trying to get out. The bars held. Increasingly desperate, he reached through the bars and pressed against the window itself. It would not budge.

Thoroughly defeated, he turned around. Only then did he see that right below him on the porch was another animal. He was a good deal bigger than Ereth, with short brown fur and small, round, dark eyes, which, to look at them, were almost blank of emotion.

"Got you," said Marty the pine marten. "Got you at last."

25
What Happened at the Cabin

Open-mouthed, Ereth stared at the pine marten.

"You thought you were being clever, hiding with those cubs for so long," Marty sneered. "But you're too stupid to know that I'm the most patient creature in the world. I've waited and watched every move you made. I saw you pretending to take care of those foxes when all you were doing was hiding from me. I saw you rush through the woods and take an indirect route back here. I saw and I followed. I'm like death. You can't escape me!

"You coward!" he went on. "I know you for what you are. You're an old, witless, selfish porcupine. But now you're going to get what you deserve. Get down from there!"

"But . . . but . . . *why?*" a very frightened Ereth stammered. "Why are you so angry at me? What did I do to you?"

"You porcupines think you can go and do anything you want," Marty replied angrily. "You're nothing but self-centred beasts without any feeling for any-one but yourselves. You don't care what you say or do. You think nothing of others. You think your quills will keep you safe. Well, I'm here to show you, porcu-pine, no one can be safe from Marty the pine marten. Not even you. Now get down!"

"But . . . but . . . I'm not like other porcupines," Ereth stammered. "Or if I was, I've changed. I've become different. I have feelings. I *do* care what others think."

"Liar!" Marty snarled. "Come on down here and get what you deserve!"

Ereth, knowing perfectly well what the pine marten could do to him, remained where he was. While he could put up resistance, he was hardly in a place to do so. Beyond that, he was exhausted from his long, difficult trek back to the cabin.

He looked around. The barred window was behind him. No escaping that way. Nor was there any escape right or left. He glanced beyond the porch, toward the woods. There, perhaps, lay safety. If he could climb into a tree he might be able to defend himself. But first he had to get to the tree, and the new snow would be slippery, perhaps even deep in places.

"Get down!" Marty shouted, eyes cold and hard. "Get down or I'll yank you down!" So saying, he reared back on his hind legs as though ready to attack.

"Mouldering mouse marbles!" Ereth cried. "I don't deserve this. I don't!" But when he saw the pine marten's muscles tense, he knew he had no choice. He had to reach the trees.

Terrified, Ereth did what he had never done in his entire life. He made a flying leap off the windowsill. Kicking back hard, he sailed over the pine marten's head, landing with a hard thump on the porch.

Marty, caught by surprise, swung around.

Paws smarting from a painful landing, a dazed Ereth struggled to his feet. He spun about, trembling with panic, and waved his quilled tail wildly, ready to smack Marty across the face if he got too close.

Marty stepped back spryly.

Seeing that he had won a brief advantage, Ereth turned again. He tried to get off the porch by running but completely forgot about the steps. Missing the first one, he tumbled head over tail, doing three complete somersaults before landing on his back in the snow, belly exposed.

Shrieking with rage, Marty extended his claws

and took a great leap off the porch, aiming right at the porcupine. Ereth saw him coming and rolled over, but not fast enough. The pine marten managed to snare him with his front claws, leaving two long scratches across Ereth's belly. Blood began to flow.

"Potato pip paste!" Ereth screamed. "I'm being murdered! Help!" He continued his roll, then turned again, once more putting his tail between himself and the snarling pine marten.

Marty, alert to the danger, backed off.

A frantic Ereth began to race toward the trees, taking what were for him great bounding leaps. As he went he trailed streaks of blood, which were like stitch marks on the white snow.

The pine marten saw where Ereth was heading. With a burst of speed he shot past the porcupine, made a sharp U-turn, and confronted him head-on.

Ereth came to a skidding stop. He started to turn, but saw that if he did, the pine marten would be herding him right back toward the cabin, the last place Ereth wanted to be.

"Give up, you stupid beast," Marty taunted. "You don't have a chance!"

"You occupational ignoramus!" Ereth screeched,

huffing and puffing as he tried to recover his breath. His heart was hammering so hard it was making him dizzy.

Trying to defend himself, he tucked his head down between his front legs, shaping himself into a ball of bristling quills. Then, with mincing steps, he awkwardly waddled forward. This moved him toward Marty, but with his head so low he could no longer see where he was going.

Marty, seeing that Ereth was attacking blindly, backed up and quickly circled the porcupine, looking for a place to attack. Noticing that the quills along Ereth's side were flattened, he leaped forward, both front paws out, trying to knock Ereth off balance.

Hit hard where he least expected it, Ereth rolled away. Once again his belly was exposed. Once again, the pine marten struck, drawing more blood.

The pain was enough to force Ereth to uncoil himself. He had to see where he was, had to see where the pine marten was, had to know how to escape. But when he looked about he was so confused and woozy he couldn't find his enemy. Belatedly, he saw that the pine marten had jumped in front of him again. Even as Ereth realised his whereabouts, Marty attacked, this time aiming right at Ereth's face.

The porcupine ducked. He avoided the worst but received a bad scrape on one ear even as he managed to butt the pine marten hard, hoping he'd poked him with a couple of quills.

Marty dropped back, coolly trying to decide where to attack next.

In that moment, Ereth stole a quick glance to see how far he was from the trees. He had covered half the distance, but it felt as if they were still miles away.

As Ereth struggled to decide what to do, Marty took another hard lunge at him, trying to knock him over. This time he missed completely and went sprawling in deep snow.

Sensing his opportunity, Ereth hurled himself toward the trees. He was beginning to think he was going to make it, when he received a hard smash on the left side.

The stroke came so suddenly, so intensely, Ereth landed hard against an old stump, the wind knocked completely out of him.

Feeling increasing pain and growing even more muddled, Ereth knew that he must get up and defend himself.

He could not.

The best he could manage was to open his eyes. He beheld a dreadful sight. Marty the pine marten was crouching a few feet away. His face bore a cruel grin. "Now I have you," Marty hissed.

"Help!" Ereth gasped. "Help!"

"You're done, porcupine," Marty snarled. "Completely *done*. No one, absolutely no one, escapes Marty the pine marten."

Ereth strained to get up again. The pain was too great. He was too weak. He was bleeding too much. "Please," he bleated. "I need some help . . . please. Someone help me."

As Marty the pine marten prepared his final, fatal spring, Ereth closed his eyes. "Goodbye, Poppy," he whispered. "Farewell, cubs!"

He opened his eyes to see the pine marten, claws fully extended, leaping at him.

The next instant there was an explosion of red. It seemed to come from nowhere, and yet it was everywhere all at once. Thinking it was his own blood he was seeing, Ereth squeezed his eyes shut. Then he heard the yelping, barking, and snarling.

Ereth opened his eyes and blinked with astonishment.

Tumble, Nimble, and Flip had burst from the woods and leaped upon the pine marten, taking him completely by surprise. What's more, they were pummeling him with all the ferocity they could muster.

Tumble, with jaws tightly clamped, was holding on to the scruff of the pine marten's neck and shaking hard, all the while grunting and snarling. Nimble had taken a fast hold of one of the pine marten's legs and was refusing to let go, no matter how much the beast thrashed. As for Flip, he had a firm grip on the pine marten's tail and was growling and yanking and pulling with all his might.

In seconds it was Marty the pine marten who was on his back, kicking and clawing frantically, trying to get away.

A weak, dazed Ereth could only mutter, "Welcome the wombats and bless all bees!"

Suddenly Marty the pine marten gave a mighty yank and freed his leg from Nimble's grasp. Though Tumble was still clinging to him and Flip refused to let go, the pine marten staggered to his feet. With a violent shake, he flung Tumble away. Then he turned and snapped savagely at Flip, who was forced to let go of the pine marten's tail.

Free at last, Marty, instead of staying to fight, whirled about, leaped through the bushes, and fled among the trees.

The cubs, tongues lolling, chests heaving, watched him go. So did Ereth. For a moment there was nothing to hear but the sound of the pine marten smashing through the underbrush. Next there came the distinct, dreadful sound of a metallic *snap*.

26

Marty the pine marten

No one moved. Not Ereth. Not Tumble, Nimble, or Flip. Instead, they all stared in the direction that Marty the pine marten had gone.

"What . . . happened?" Nimble said at last, though she as well as everybody else was pretty sure.

Tumble, trembling visibly, began to edge forward, his nose extended, sniffing.

"Careful!" Ereth cried out from where he lay. "There may be more traps about. When I checked, there were none left under the cabin."

"Do you think he got . . . caught?" Flip asked.

No one replied. Instead, the three cubs crept forward into the brush. Hauling himself up, Ereth limped painfully along.

"Look!" Tumble cried. He had managed to get ahead of the others.

The two other cubs went forward. Ereth came last.

What they saw was the large box trap from

under the cabin. Inside — very much alive — was Marty the pine marten. In his haste to get away he had rushed blindly into it. The moment he did, the doors at either end snapped shut.

The three cubs and Ereth crept closer, their eyes glued to the sight.

Marty, his face bearing a look of terrible rage, glared out at them. "Don't just stand there gawking," he snarled. "Get me out of here!"

Neither Ereth nor the cubs replied.

"You don't understand," the caged animal said, speaking with barely suppressed fury. "I'm from the great pine marten family. No finer animals in all the world. We've been hunted down everywhere by humans because of our fur. Even dolts like you must be capable of seeing how beautiful I am. We're so beautiful there are very few pine martens left. Every time one of us is killed or captured, the chances of our survival are reduced. Now, get the cage open."

"But . . . you were trying to kill Ereth!" Nimble protested.

"Of course I was," returned the pine marten.

"But . . . why should you want to do that?" Flip asked.

"Because," returned Marty proudly, "only pine martens are smart enough to deal with porcupines. Now stop yapping and open the trap!"

The cubs looked to Ereth.

"I . . . don't know how to open it," Ereth said.

"You blundering idiot!" Marty the pine marten cried out. "Can't you do anything right? Open your eyes. There's a rod lever on top. Push it down. It'll open the trap doors. The four of you can do it easily."

Once again the three cubs looked to Ereth, waiting for him to decide.

"Fumigated goat fidgets," Ereth muttered, not knowing what to do.

"Will . . . you promise not to hurt Ereth?" Tumble asked.

"And just go away and leave us alone?" Nimble added.

"I don't make deals with anyone," the pine marten shouted. "Just get me out!"

The cubs turned yet again to Ereth.

Ereth sighed deeply. He could feel the pain where the pine marten had clawed him. And yet, as he looked at the beast in the trap, all he could think of was the pine marten's predicament. "Frog freckles," he grumbled. "I suppose we should."

"Of course you should," Marty snarled. "The weak always have an obligation to help the strong. We're the important ones. Besides, I've suffered a great deal. Didn't I just explain? You have an obligation to help me."

Lumbering forward, Ereth approached the cage. After sniffing and studying it carefully, he found the bar Marty had mentioned, the one that would open the trap. Rearing up he pushed down on it. It gave way partly but not enough to release the doors. He looked around at the cubs. "Come on," he called.

"Ereth . . ." Flip called, "are . . . you sure we should do this?"

"Come on," Ereth growled, "lend a paw!"

Tumble jumped atop the trap. Nimble reared up from one side, while Flip got close to Ereth.

"When I say three, we'll all push," Ereth said.

"Would you hurry!" Marty snarled.

"One . . . two . . ." Ereth stopped.

From somewhere in the distance came a high-pitched whine.

Tumble cocked his ears. "What's that?"

The animals listened.

"Faster, you fools!" Marty shouted. "I must get out!"

The whine grew louder, becoming a growl as it got closer.

"What is that?" Flip asked Ereth.

"Pig pudding," the porcupine swore. "It's the snowmobile. The hunters. They're coming back."

"Let me out of here!" Marty shrieked. "Don't let them get me. You mustn't!"

The sound of the snowmobile grew very loud.

Ereth leaped off the trap. "Into the woods!" he cried to the cubs. "Hide! Run!" He scrambled away painfully.

The cubs tore after him.

"Don't leave me!" Marty screamed. "Don't let them get me!"

Ereth dove under the low-lying branches of a pine tree. The cubs quickly joined him.

"What's going to happen?" a frightened Flip asked.

"Shut up!" Ereth ordered.

The four peered out through the tree branches. They could still see the trap. Marty was thrashing about, trying desperately to free himself.

The sound of the snowmobile had become a roar. The next moment they saw it burst into the clearing in front of the cabin and stop. It was the same machine Ereth had seen before. Sure enough, two men were perched on it. Though they were so bundled up it was hard to see their faces, Ereth recognized the furs they were wearing: they were the same humans he'd dealt with before.

Sure enough, one of them said, "Hey, Wayne, look here. There's blood on the ground."

The man on the backseat leaped off and peered into the snow. "Some animal has been wounded," he said.

"That's my blood, you two-legged lump of wind cheese!" Ereth snarled.

"Shut up!" Tumble whispered.

Ereth gave the fox a dirty look but said no more.

"Whatever it was, it went this way," said the man. He began to follow the trail of Ereth's blood away from the cabin, moving right to the stump where the struggle had taken place. The other man followed.

"Look here, Parker," the first man said. "Must have been some kind of fight. Must have been a whole bunch of animals."

"Tracks go there," the man named Parker said. He began to move toward the trap.

Ereth and the three cubs, not even daring to breathe, watched.

"Wayne," Parker called. "I think we got something."

"Good Lord . . . what is it?"

"Not certain. Look at that gorgeous fur. But he sure is mad. Watch out for his claws."

"Hey, that's a pine marten!"

"Cool!"

"Lot better than that porcupine we were trying to get. Zoo material. Might give us a lot for it."

The two men picked up the trap and began to walk toward the cabin. Once they reached it they opened the door and took the trap inside with them. Then they closed the door with a bang.

At first the animals under the tree said nothing. It was Flip who finally spoke.

Turning to Ereth, he nudged him with his wet nose. "Are you all right?" he asked.

"Did you hear what he said?" Ereth muttered. "They were trying to catch *me*!"

"Ereth," Flip repeated, "is your body all right?"

"Oh. Some cuts and bruises. Where did you all come from?"

"The den," Tumble said.

"But . . . your father . . . where is he?"

"Dad?" Flip said. There was a slight look of embarrassment about his face. "He said he had some business to do."

"And he *left*?" Ereth asked, feeling his indignation rise.

"It's okay. He asked us if we minded being left alone," Nimble explained. "We said we didn't."

"He said he only came back to be sure you weren't bothering us," Tumble said.

Flip said, "So the day after you left, he took off."

"It was important business," Tumble interjected with some of his old heat.

"But . . . when will he be coming back?" Ereth asked.

"Oh, sometime in the spring," Nimble said casually.

"Right. He's going to take us hunting," Tumble said.

"He's really great at that," Flip put in.

Ereth thought of saying something. Instead he told them, "You saved my life. And . . . and I didn't think I'd ever see you again."

"You didn't?" Flip said, taken by surprise. "Why?"

"Because . . . oh, toe jam on a toothbrush," Ereth grumbled. "I just didn't, that's all."

"I mean," Nimble said, "Dad is fun, but you're the one who takes care of us. So of course you'd have to see us again."

"The thing is," Tumble added in his sour way, "Dad has more important things to do than take care of cubs. But Ereth, you're so old you've got nothing better to do."

A speechless Ereth looked around.

"So can you come back to the den with us?" Nimble asked.

Ereth glowered.

"We found the last trap," Tumble said. "You won't have to worry about that."

"Will you come back?" Flip coaxed.

"No," Ereth said at last.

"*No?*" the cubs chorused.

"I'm going home. My home."

"But . . . what about . . . *us?*" Flip whispered.

"You'll be fine without me," Ereth said. "You didn't eat up all that food your mother left you, did you?"

"No."

"Good. It should get you through the winter."

The dismayed foxes stared at Ereth.

"But . . . we'll miss you," Nimble said.

"A lot," Flip said.

To which Tumble added, "Yeah, we will."

"Tumbled toad toes," Ereth grumbled. He looked out through the forest and toward the south — and his home.

"Ereth . . ." Flip said. "Guess what?"

"What?"

"There was something we forgot to tell you."

"What's that?"

Flip looked from Nimble, to Tumble, then back to Ereth. "We wanted to say . . . thank you."

The pain in Ereth's chest was making it hard for him to breathe. "Oh, bobcat beads," he muttered.

"And another thing," Tumble said.

"Stop!" Ereth snapped. "I don't want to hear!"

"We . . . like you. A lot."

Ereth looked away.

"And anyway," Nimble added, "I bet with those scratches that pine marten gave you, you'll need us to look after you. Am I right?"

"Right," Flip said, "this time we'll take care of you."

Ereth stared at the three cubs, who were sitting in a row. Tongues lolling, eyes full of bright curiosity, large-eared and big-pawed, they seemed so terribly young.

"Bug bottoms," Ereth muttered. "You'll never be able to take care of me."

"But if you don't let us try," Nimble said, "you won't ever know, will you?"

"Yeah," Tumble said.

"Centipede armpits!" Ereth cried. "All I want is to go back to my own smelly log."

The cubs looked at one another. It was Flip who said, "Well, then we'll go with you."

"No!"

"But . . . why not?" Flip said.

"If you came to my place, what would you eat?"

"What we always do," Tumble said. "Meat."

"Look here, nibble nose, my best friends are mice."

"Oh," Nimble said.

"If you so much as touch one whisker of one mouse — *one!* — I'll turn you inside out so fast you won't know what direction you're going. If you come with me for a visit you're going to eat nothing but . . . but vegetables."

The foxes exchanged looks.

Tumble grinned. "That's okay with us," he said. "But only when we visit you."

27

Ereth's Birthday

Ereth led the way, the three foxes trotting by his side. With the porcupine limping, they moved slowly. Now and again the foxes darted off, but they never went far and they always came back.

At first they chatted quite a bit, asking Ereth questions about where he lived, how he lived, whom he lived with, along with countless queries about Poppy. Ereth answered very little. To most questions, he said, "You'll see." Or, "None of your business, nit nose."

So the foxes chatted among themselves. It was continual, it was loud, and was not without some bickering. Ereth paid little mind, but waddled slowly, steadily on.

It had taken one day for Ereth to come from his home to Long Lake. The return trip took two days. There were moments he felt he should just turn around and go with the foxes to their den. But he kept reminding himself that he wanted to be in his own dark and smelly home. He also needed to see Poppy.

Of course, as he limped along, he occasionally thought about the salt he'd left behind in the cabin. Perhaps someday he would go back. But as he mused on when that day might be he suddenly stopped.

"What's the matter?" Flip asked him.

"I'm very old," Ereth whispered. Though he found himself glancing over his shoulder from time to time, he said no more.

They arrived home the following day just about noon. It was Columbine, playing about at the foot of the snag, who first saw them coming.

"Uncle Ereth!" she cried with delight. "You're back!"

"Of course I'm back, you dull dab of bobcat widdle. Where else would I be?"

"But . . . you've been gone so . . ." Then Columbine saw the three foxes. Frightened, she turned tail and raced into the snag.

In moments Poppy ran out. She was joined by Rye and the rest of the litter. "Ereth," Poppy cried, "where have you been?"

Ereth wanted to burst out with all that had happened. Instead he said, "Oh, busy."

"But you were gone for a *month*. We were worried."

"You were?"

"Of course we were." Poppy looked over to the three foxes. "Are these friends of yours?"

"Absolutely. This is Tumble, Nimble, and Flip. Cubs, this is Poppy. And her husband, Rye. These mice are named Columbine, Mariposa, Snowberry, Walnut, Verbena, Scrub-oak, Pipsissewa, Crabgrass, Locust, Sassafras, and Ragweed the Second."

"How-do-you-do-Tumble-Nimble-and-Flip," the young mice chorused.

Rye considered the foxes nervously. "Are they . . . safe?" he asked Ereth.

"Strict vegetarians."

"Oh, okay."

The foxes, remembering all the tales Ereth had told, gazed at the famous Poppy with awe. She was so small, but she had done so much!

It was Poppy who said, "Ereth, did you realise that on the day you went off, it was your birthday?"

"Is that so?" Ereth replied, trying not to frown. "I suppose I forgot."

Sassafras ran over to Poppy and whispered into her ear, "Ma! Ereth's . . . you know."

"Oh, my, yes," Poppy said. "You really should."

With that all eleven of the young mice raced back into the hole at the base of the snag.

"It's just a little something Rye and I – and the children – got for your birthday," Poppy explained. "We went to get it for you that morning."

Ereth could feel himself blushing. "Well, it didn't seem to me that . . ."

"The children said they tried to get you to stay but you rushed off."

The young mice reappeared, rolling forward a large lump of salt. The lump being six times the size of any one of the youngsters, all of whom were trying to be helpful, there was much slipping and falling, squeaking and laughing.

"Happy birthday, Uncle Ereth!" they cried in unison when they finally reached the porcupine.

It was Rye who explained: "You see, Ereth, Poppy and I got it from the salt block at New Farm. Unfortunately, it took us longer to drag it back than we thought it would. By the time we got home you had gone."

"And we had no idea where," Poppy added.

"Then the storm came," Rye said.

"We began to think something might have

happened to you," Poppy went on. "Really, Ereth, we were very worried. But we didn't know where to look. When you go off that way you really must leave some word. I . . . I began to think something awful happened to you. I've been very upset."

Eyes glued to the gift, Ereth stood there open-mouthed, incapable of saying a word. "*Salt . . .*" he muttered finally, already drooling.

"Speech, Uncle Ereth," Sassafras cried. "Birthday boys have to make speeches."

Ereth took a deep breath. "I . . . Oh, pull the chain and grab five mops," he managed to say, even as tears began to roll down his cheeks. "I . . . don't know what to say," he muttered between sobs, "except . . . oh, thank you . . . thank each and every one of you."

The next moment the eleven young mice started to sing "Happy Birthday" in a very ragged chorus. The three foxes joined in with howls of their own.

Ereth could not wait until they were done. He snatched up the salt and began to lick it in a frenzy of delight.

The mice cheered. The foxes bayed.

And if Ereth's tears made the salt a little saltier than usual, that might explain why, as far as the old porcupine was concerned, it was the best-tasting salt he had ever eaten in his whole, long life.

Indeed, as the years went by and Ereth grew truly old and his quills became grey — and less sharp — and he looked back on all that had happened to him, he had no doubt — not the slightest doubt in all the world — that this birthday turned out to be the very best he'd ever had.

About the Author

Avi was born in 1937 in the city of New York. His twin sister gave him this name when they were both about a year old, and it stuck.

He has written over fifty highly acclaimed books for children, including *Crispin*, which won the prestigious Newbery Medal. *Ereth's Birthday* is the third book of his celebrated Dimwood Forest Chronicles; also available are *Poppy*, *Poppy and Rye* and *Ragweed*.